Other Titles by this Author;

Pools of Unheard Tears

The Cold Hand of Fate

Chaotic Inertia

When the Beat Stops, Then I die

In the Crosshairs of Death

A Bed Full of Vipers

Hell is Best

Served

Ice Cold

1

"That was a bloody good get-together at Jodie's house, wasn't it?" said Bruce, as he and Chloe his wife of seven years, turned off the main road and onto the long narrow country lane.

Bruce Parker was a high flyer in the City of London, where he worked as a Merchant banker. His wife Chloe was a Head Teacher at a nearby primary school. They had moved to live in the area, about two years ago after she'd been promoted to Head Teacher. They both adored living in the quiet of the countryside, after moving away from the hustle and bustle of the big city. Now though the overhanging trees swayed about in front of them. Blown about by an icy biting wind that made the now bare branches, rub against each other creating a moaning sound, as if they were saying that winter was not too far away. The dark twisting lane wound around the trunks of trees hiding individual animals that were zigzagging, across the dark lane, still collecting their harvest of food to see them through the cold times to come. Many a time they would leave it almost too late to scurry away out of the cars headlights and the imminent death that the car's tyres would bring to if they were ever to make contact with one of them. Dead leaves rustled and small twigs danced erratically across the road in front of them, occasionally; something would hit the side of the car making both of them jump. It was by now almost two thirty in the morning and after having a few drinks, they were both feeling the wrong side of keeping awake.

Turning onto this dark lane however, meant that they were not too, far from the warmth and comfort of their own home.

"God, I'm glad that tomorrow is Saturday, at least I know that soon, I'll be able to sleep off the remnants of this evening," yawned Bruce, as they turned a sharp bend in the lane.

However, before Chloe could reply, she suddenly screamed, "Look out!" pointing ahead of them.

Bruce, although not seeing anything himself, automatically slammed his foot down hard on the brake pedal, making the car screech to a halt, forcing both of their bodies hard against the seatbelts.

"What the hell! Why did you shout out like that?" said Bruce, who by now was beginning to shake.

"There was a little child standing in the road!" said Chloe as she scanned the road in front of the car.

Bruce opened the car door and got out for a better look. "I can't see a child," said Bruce, looking at the area that was being lit up by the cars headlights.

"But I saw her," shouted Chloe getting out of the car herself. "Oh God, you didn't hit her did we?"

"What the hell would a child be doing out at this time of night on her own, it's crazy!" said Bruce as he stared out into the lane. With only the car headlights supplying any form of light. His ability to see around his vehicle was greatly restricted because his eyes were struggling to refocus, as they moved from the light to the pitch-blackness.

Bruce reached back inside the car and took a small torch out of the car's glove box. Then he told his wife to come with him to the rear of the car. Both as an extra pair of eyes and the fact that he didn't feel too comfortable being out in the dark and isolated lane at this time of night!

Now he had the torch turned on, they both scanned the roadway looking for any sign of the little girl, but there was none.

"Look it's friggin freezing out here," said Bruce as he rubbed his hands up and down on his arms to aid the body's circulation. "You must have been imagining it, let's get back in the car and give the police a call if you're still convinced that you saw her when we get home."

Bruce then made a beeline for the driver's door and warmth of the heater inside the car, while Chloe, who was still looking all around, made her way back towards the passenger side of the car. Bruce had just closed his door to when he heard Chloe give out a loud scream!

Bruce immediately jumped back out of the car and raced round to where his wife was standing. "What the hell's the matter with you?" shouted Bruce when he got closer to where his wife's was standing.

"Look!" said Chloe, as she bent down. Bruce shone his torch on the ground in front of Chloe and saw lying on the freezing tarmac, the body of a very young girl.

"Is she alive?" asked Bruce nervously, not knowing if he'd actually hit her or not.

Chloe cautiously reached out and felt her small neck to see if she could feel a pulse. "Yes, she's still alive but for how long, that I don't know. Her little body is stone cold!"

"I'm not surprised," replied Bruce looking down at her. "I mean, she's only wearing a thin dress and she's not even wearing any socks or shoes on her feet!"

"Pick her up and give her to me when I get in the car," said Chloe, standing up and moving quickly to get inside the car

Bruce stooped down, scooped up the ice-cold body of the little girl and carried her to the car. He then handed her over to his wife Chloe, who carefully cradled her in her arms and then wrapped her coat around the pair of them and switched on the car's heater to full power. It was then that Chloe noticed that the front and back of the little girl's leg's, were covered in dried blood. She gingerly lifted up her lightweight tattered dress to see if there were any other injuries visible. That was when she noticed several cuts stretching from her feet right up to the girl's thighs. Some of these had actually punctured her skin resulting in the blood loss.

  Chloe then began to wonder why a child so young would be out here on her own and how did she get to have all these cuts to her lower body. It was at that point, Bruce rushed back and after memorising where in the lane, they were. Started the car's engine and raced off back to the warmth of their house. Once there, while Chloe tried to keep the child warm and comfort her. She resisted trying to clean the girl's wounds in case they could provide police with any clues and help them to discover what had happened to her. Chloe's mind then began to run riot, as she visualised all different scenarios that could have resulted in these types of injuries. Her husband Bruce in the meantime, called the police and ambulance services and told them what had happened. As he put down the phone, Chloe called him across to her and carefully lift the girls dress and showed her bloodstained legs to him.

"Do you think I hit her?" he asked Chloe, sounding horrified at the thought.

"No I don't," replied Chloe, trying hard to reassure him. "I think these injuries are from being cut with something like a knife or something like that!"

"Oh shit, do you think there's a nutter out there in the woods?" replied Bruce, as he went and looked out through the window into the darkness of the night.

"Let's leave what cased this to the police shall we," replied Chloe knowing that bravery was not Bruce's forte.

"Go and get some warm towels for me out of the airing cupboard will you Bruce, so I can wrap her up in them until help arrives," called Chloe as she pulled her chair closer to the fireplace where the imitation log fire was flickering into life.

Soon Bruce appeared with a bundle of warm bath towels and he helped Chloe wrap the child in them so that only her dirty pale face was visible.

"Shall I make us all a hot drink?" asked Bruce feeling lost as to what to do for the best.

"Yes dear, you do that while I try to get some warmth into her," replied Chloe holding the little girl close to her chest.

While they waited by the warmth of the fire for the police and ambulance to arrive. They sat there drinking some hot cocoa and wondering what was this child doing out there in the first place.

It was around fifteen minutes later when blue flashing lights lit up the darkness of the night outside their property. Bruce wasted no time in opening up the front door and ushering the ambulance personnel into the lounge where his wife was sitting. One of the paramedics reached down to take the child from Chloe. However, as he touched her, the little girl's eyes opened briefly and when she saw him, she reached out with shaking hands and gripped Chloe's clothing tightly. Her young face and body began to shake as she turned and nestled her face into Chloe's breast but was that just from the cold or was she frightened.

"It's alright little one," said Chloe softly into the child's ear. "He's here to help you, not to hurt you."

When the little girl heard those words of reassurance, she gave a little smile and then released her grip on Chloe's cardigan. She handed the child over to them so that they could run some health checks on her. It was at that point that Chloe quietly told the paramedic about the bloodstains on her legs. He gave Chloe a brief smile and reassured her that they would be taking very good care of her. After checking her over, they assessed her age to be about five. As soon as their checks were completed, they got her ready for transportation to hospital. The paramedic then wrapped her up in a big white blanket that they had brought in from the ambulance. Chloe, bent down gave her a kiss on her cheek and told her not to be afraid.

A few minutes later, a police car turned up and two police officers entered the property. Bruce and Chloe gave a statement to the officers as to how they discovered her lying in the road. A few minutes later, the ambulance left the Parkers home for the hospital. Before they left however, the paramedic that dealt with the child reassured the Parkers that their interaction had probably saved the child from a severe case of hypothermia.

The two police officers then asked Bruce if he would show them exactly where they had discovered the little girl. He was pleased to assist them and promptly put on a warm coat prior to getting into the back of the police car. At the precise spot in the lane where they had found her, all three men got out of the car. Bruce nervously remained with the car, while the two officers using powerful torches, proceeded to take a quick look around. Their immediate intention was to search the area for any sign of the child's mother or father, or any sign of her socks and shoes. However, after a fruitless search, they radioed their position back to the control room and waited for extra manpower to arrive, so that they could construct a more substantial search of the area.

Bruce, was hitherto returned home, as soon as extra personnel began to arrive. The search however was called off, after twelve hours of searching the wooded area, without finding anything that could help them to identify who, the missing child was?

With nothing else to go on, the case of the child with no name, was handed over to the child protection agency. They were much better equipped than the police to take care of her immediate needs while she is in hospital.

2

Detective Chief Inspector Dave Geraint of the Serious Crime Squad located in London's New Scotland Yard was this morning for the first time in ages enjoying pottering about in his front garden. It was that time of the year, when things had or were dying down and they needed ripping out before the ground became too hard to pull up, when someone called out his name? With a sigh, he turned around and was surprised to see Detective Constable Sam Parsons, his partner at the Yard standing there.

"What the hell are you doing here and on a Saturday of all days?" said Dave reluctantly.

"Sorry sir, but I tried your phone and got no reply so I decided to come round myself," replied Sam who was half expecting a bollocking for disturbing his boss's day off.

"Oh go on then, what's happened now?" said Dave, realising that his day in the garden was over before it had ever begun.

"Someone has lost a security van and they want us, I mean you to look for it," said Sam.

"How the fuck, do you lose one of those things, don't they have trackers or something like that fitted to prevent this sort of thing?" snapped Dave.

"Yes they do have those types of things fitted and that's the problem. From what I've learnt so far and that ain't much, the van was towards the end of its collections for the day prior to them returning to the firms secure site, when the alarm was activated. They tried to make contact with the vehicle but were not successful. However, it did register on their virtual mapping system, where and on which road the vehicle was when the alarm was originally activated. They immediately contacted the local police force and units were hastily dispatched to that exact spot. But on arrival there was no sign of the missing van or the guards, and the firm informed the police that the van's security signal was no longer emitting their position," said Sam.

"And you say that the police that attended the spot where it had been found nothing?" said Dave as he gathered up his hand tools and made his way towards the garden shed.

"Nothing!" replied Sam. "There were no witnesses, tyre tracks or in fact anything to say that anything had happened there at all!"

"So why do they think we can do any better than the local coppers, if there's nothing more for us to go on than they had?" replied Dave, locking up his shed. "Oh, alright I'm just having a moan. Give me fifteen minutes and I'll be with you. Where have you got the car?"

"Oh it's that one parked in front of your front gate sir!" replied Sam sarcastically.

"Smart arse!" replied Dave with a half smile. "See you in a mo." Disappearing inside his front door.

Less than thirty minutes later, Dave reappeared suited and booted ready for work.

"Well, where are we off to then?" asked Dave as he climbed into the passenger side of the car.

"If it's alright with you sir, I thought that we'd head across to the security office and start from there?" replied Sam.

"Well, we've got to start somewhere so why not there," said Dave putting on his seat belt.

"By the way, what's this company called?"

Sam flicked through his notes and replied,

"Robert Barnes Securities, the Director and manager of the company is also the owner, a Mr Robert Barnes."

"And where are they based?" said Dave, trying to get his head into a work mode.

"According to this, they are situated on a small industrial site just off the A13 at Ratcliff."

"Right then, let them know that were on the way and let's give their tree a shake and see what falls out shall we!" replied Dave as they pulled out into the traffic.

It took them only half an hour to reach the security firm. On their arrival they were met by Mr Barnes himself, who showed them through to his office.

"Thank you for coming so quickly," said Mr Barnes as he gestured them both to sit down.

"I am DCI Geraint and this is DC Parsons, tell me what exactly happened prior to losing one of your vans?"

"Well, all of our vehicles are equipped with the latest tracking device. That then enables the control room staff to monitor their routes. Should there be a problem with any of the vehicles and it's alarm is activated. It automatically flashes up on the screen and an alarm rings to attract the controller's attention," said Mr Barnes.

"So what went wrong?" asked Sam taking notes.

"Nothing, nothing went wrong," replied Mr Barnes defensively. "Why do you imply that something went wrong?"

"Well, you say that as soon as the alarm was activated, the police were informed. They immediately dispatched a unit to the co-ordinates that your controller gave them but when they arrived, there was no sign of the security van. As I asked before, what went wrong?" said Sam looking directly at Mr Barnes.

"Look, I think that you would be better asking the controllers that question as they were on duty when the alarm was raised," said Mr Barnes standing up.

With a sly wink to Sam, Dave stood up and they both followed the slightly rattled owner through to the control room. As they entered the control room, they were met with a dimly lit room that had a huge plasma screen situated on the wall in front of a raised desk that housed the radio equipment.

"Peter, Simon, these gentlemen are police officers and they are here to ask questions about the missing van. I want you to tell them anything that they need to know, ok!" said Mr Barnes as he stood to one side.

"Hello, I'm DCI Geraint and this is DC Parsons, sorry you are?"

"Oh I'm Peter Conway and I'm Simon Hewitt," replied the two controllers.

For the next thirty minutes, the two men advised how the system in front of them worked and the procedure in place should there be an attack on one of the vehicles. They also advised Dave of the pre-agreed route that the security vehicle should take.

"Do they always keep to the set route or are there sometimes changes made and if so how do they communicate that to you?" asked Dave.

"Most of the time the route never changes, however say for instance they needed to alter their route. Say for instance a road closure or road works where there was going to be long delays. They would then transmit that to us via a pre-arranged code that we have for pickups. In that way, if someone were monitoring the radio wavelength, then they would have no idea which code represented which premise. So they would not be able to intercept the van en-route," explained Simon.

"Tell me, were both of you on duty when the van went missing?" asked Dave as he looked around the room.

"Yes sir," replied Simon. "There are always two of us working in here so that if one of us needs the loo, then there is always one of us here to cover should anything go wrong."

"And when you had the alarm, you immediately contacted the police and informed them of the potential problem!" asked Dave watching both of the men intently.

"Yes," replied Peter immediately looking across to his colleague. "Why do you ask that?"

"Oh no reason," replied Dave shrugging his shoulders. "It's just the kind of thing I like to ask. It helps me get a better picture of the working practices, that's all. Oh Mr Barnes, I wonder while I'm having a chat in here, would you show DC Parsons one of your vehicles. Tin that way we will have a better knowledge of the size of the vehicle and the set up inside. Is that ok?"

Mr Barnes gave Dave a nod and moved towards the doorway. Dave in the meantime, walked across and whispered something into Sam's ear. He then gave a short nod of the head and left the room with Mr Barnes.

"So, is this place fully self sufficient, or do you have to leave the room if one of you needs the loo?" asked Dave, in a more relaxed tone of voice.

"No, we have everything that we need in here without having to leave one of us on our own," replied Peter.

"That's good," said Dave calmly. "Now would you both write down for me what you were both doing when the van's alarm was activated?"

"Yes, we can do that for you sir," said Simon as he passed a sheet of paper across to Peter and they, both began writing.

A few minutes later the door to the control room opened up and Mr Barnes and Sam re-entered the room.

"Everything ok," asked Dave to Sam.

"Sam did not reply but just gave Dave the thumbs up and smiled.

"Mr Barnes I wonder if you could tell me what that red flashing light is?" said Dave pointing towards the plasma screen on the wall.

"What, how can this be?" he replied when he looked up at the screen. "That's a vehicle alarm going off, but why is there no sound?"

That last ranting statement brought the two controllers back to reality and both looked up at the screen and saw the red flashing light.

"Shit, there's an alarm gone off, quick which van is in trouble?" said Peter as he and Simon focused on the read out that was above the flashing red light. "Hang on a minute, that van's still in the compound. What's going on here?"

Dave, who had watched the two controller's reaction closely when the alarm was eventually drawn to their attention. Was secretly impressed with the speed that they found out where the alarm was coming from.

"Ah that would be down to me I'm afraid," said Dave. "I asked my DC to set off an alarm in one of the vehicles if he got the chance. I was interested in how quick your responses were when an alarm was triggered."

"Yes that's ok," replied Peter who was still calming down from the shock. "But it doesn't answer why there was no sound emitted when the red light began to flash?"

"How often is the system tested?" asked Sam.

"Every morning, prior to the first vehicle leaving the secure compound," replied Simon as he pressed the test button for the system.

Immediately, a piercing alarm rang out making both Dave and Sam cover their ears. However as the panel reset itself from the test, the red light from the van inside the compound was still flashing.

"But how can that be," said Mr Barnes. "While they are inside the compound itself, the vehicle alarms are all set to silent. However once they pass through the electric front gates, a signal is automatically emitted, turning the sound part of the alarm back on."

"Oh so that's why there was no sound when I set it off out there in the yard. I must admit, I did wonder about that myself?" said Sam.

"Something must be wrong inside the equipment," said Mr Barnes in an agitated manner. Simon ask one of the vans that are out on patrol to press the alarm test button and see if it registers with us or not?"

Simon gave his boss a nod and then spoke over the radio. Then using a pre-arranged code, he asked the van driver to instigate a test. Within seconds of the request, a red light began to flash on the plasma screen but no sound was heard.

"We must get the engineers in and sort this problem out before anything else happens," said Mr Barnes. "Oh by the way, here is the information you requested about the team that were working on that van when it disappeared."

Sam took the folder from Mr Barnes and quickly scanned through it. "I see that there were three men assigned to the van. Why was that?"

"There are always three guards to each van," replied Mr Barnes. "There is the driver, navigator and the person who is locked in the rear. He is the one that transfers the sealed boxes holding the money into the huge safe located inside the rear of the van."

"Phew, I don't think that I'd like to be locked away like that without the option of being able to get out if I needed to!" said Sam. "By the way, tell me, how much cash would they have been carrying when they went missing?"

Mr Barnes looked at some of his paperwork and then replied, "Between, £200-£300,000 as an estimate."

"Phew, I didn't think that there was that amount of cash floating around these days, with so much plastic being used now a days," said Sam shaking his head.

"Is that the normal amount that this vehicle would carry while on this route?" asked Dave, as he watched the movements of all three men.

"Err, no, normally it would only be carrying £150-£200,000. But we were trying out a new working practice of combining the picking up of cash from supermarkets and the filling up of the ATM's at the same premises, to try to save money on the doubling up of journey times," replied Mr Barnes rather sheepishly.

"So to try to save money, your company have raised the ante on the personnel who work in those vehicles. Making them more of a target for the unscrupulous element in our society, I mean to say, you have not only raised the amount that they are carrying, but you have them waiting and more vulnerable for longer periods while they fill up the stores ATM's. Do you think that this action alone could have any bearing on the now missing security van along with its personnel?" said Dave looking directly at the boss and eagerly waiting hear his response to that statement.

Mr Barnes thought carefully before he replied, then asked Dave, "Are you implying that the men on the van had taken the money for themselves?"

"Well it would be one possible solution to them all still being missing, wouldn't it?" said Dave with an impassive sounding tone of voice.

"No, I'm sorry but I can't believe that of them. They have been very professional at their job since they came to work for me," said Mr Barnes defiantly.

"And how long is that then?" asked Sam, making Mr Barnes change his turn his head to look at him.

"Well let me see, Ted brown, has been with the firm for about nine years, I believe. Tom Sterling, eight years and Roger Pickles six. If you need the exact length of their service then I will have to get it from their personnel files," replied Mr Barnes.

"No, that won't be necessary at the moment," replied Dave. "But we will need all of their home addresses and telephone numbers so that we can have a chat with their family members if needed. Because if they didn't take the money, then their can only be one other reason why they are still missing, in my books," said Dave.

"And what's that?" demanded Mr Barnes.

"It's because they are all dead, that's why?" replied Sam. "Can you tell me again why there were three men and not the two who would normally be working these vehicles?"

"Well it has to be that way for the insurance companies to cover us. They dictated that the man in the rear of the vehicle must be locked inside the van until it returns to the safety of the firm's compound. Otherwise, he could be forced to open up from the inside, in the event that his colleagues were taken prisoner by an armed gang!" replied Mr Barnes in a matter of fact manner.

Dave listened to the boss explain the reasoning behind the companies rulings, then, he decided to try another tack. "Ok, we've digressed off the subject just a little bit. So let's get back to what we were talking about. Oh, yes, so we've established that there was more than likely a longer delay in advising the police seeing that there was no sound when the alarm was set off. What I need to know is how much longer, in the light of things could it have been?" said Dave.

Simon and Peter both shook their heads while trying to think of an answer. Then in a stroke of luck, Simon suddenly reached out for the day's logbook, which they have to record everything that occurs. "Right, we logged the alarm signal yesterday at 18.27hrs. The only log prior to that was made at 17.42hrs, when van 296a notified us that he had a flat tyre and asked us to get someone out there to change it for them."

"So that now changes the time line dramatically," said Dave, doing some mental calculations in his head. "So say that you notified the police by 18.30pm and they took twenty minutes to get there depending on traffic. That would mean that they would have arrived at the scene at, let's say for an example, 18.50hrs. Therefore, that would now give us a forty-five minute gap from the alarm to the van disappearing. Now that time frame seems much more viable that the twenty minutes that we were at first working on, doesn't it?"

"Sir, I can get all the exact timings from the local police if you need to have them," said Sam.

"Yes please, we might just need them later on if these people are half as clever as they appear to be," replied Dave. "Right then gentlemen, I don't think that we need to detain you anymore. We now have a lot more information than we did when we first arrived. Mr Barnes, will you inform either DC Parsons or myself when the fault is found? I will be interested in discovering why the vehicle alarms have all been muted in real life!"

Mr Barnes gave Dave a nod and after a quick glance around the room the two detectives were escorted back to the front of the building by him. After the cursory goodbyes, Dave and Sam headed back to their car.

"Well what do you think about that then?" said Dave as he stood next to the car and turned for another look at the building.

"If that was my business then I'd be kicking arse good and proper, until I found out what had gone wrong. That Barnes fellow seems too relaxed about the whole caper for my liking. I mean, if I'd lost a security van along with all its personnel, then I'd be climbing the wall by now wondering what had happened to it. Then, what do you say to their family members, if they have any?" said Sam.

"Mm, yes I agree it's all very interesting but something's telling me that we've only scratched the tip of this ice berg. I want to see what happens when the entire thing begins to roll over!" said Dave as they both climbed into the police car and headed back to the Yard.

3

At the map co-ordinates, the two detectives were given from Mr Barnes on their departure from his company that denoted the last position of the security van, prior to its disappearance. Dave and Sam leant on their car and scanned the surrounding area.

"This looks like an old run down industrial estate, this stretch of road is quite deserted for being not that far away from the capital. I mean, since we've been here, what's that five or so minutes. Not one car, van or lorry has come past," said Dave as he began to walk back and forth looking for something, anything that would help them solve the bizarre disappearance. "I can understand hijacking a security vehicle for its contents. However, why have the hijackers, after getting hold of what they needed, bothered, to take the bloody vehicle as well? It just doesn't make any sense!"

"Maybe they couldn't get what they needed and decided to take the van to a safer place so that they could work on it away from prying eyes?" replied Sam, trying hard to add a different aspect to their thinking.

"Mm, I would agree with the assessment of that situation except for one tiny flaw," said Dave who was still looking round.

"And that is?"

"How on earth did they manage to move the dam thing? I mean, if they couldn't, for some reason gain access to the vehicle, then how did they manage to move it? These people work on the surprise of the attack to throw the guards off their game. Are you telling me they brought along a flatbed truck, just in case they had to winch the van onto its back on the off chance they couldn't get hold of the van's contents. Surely, someone would have driven past and been a witness to them attempting that?" said Dave.

"Ah, but what if the road had been closed for some reason?" replied Sam. "I mean, it didn't have to be closed officially, they could have just put up signs stating that it was closed, couldn't they?"

Dave thought for a minute and then replied, "That, young man is a good idea of yours. What I need you to do now is to arrange for the local coppers to do a quick stop and question all the drivers that use this road and get them to ask just that type of question. If the answer bears out your theory, then we will have to start looking into how many large lorries, or flatbeds have been stolen recently. Get on to that now will you and make the arrangements, while I have a look around this site and give it the once over for my own satisfaction."

So as Sam got onto the police radio to the police control room and arranged for the road checks to begin a.s.a.p. Dave wondered off into the distant abandoned industrial site for a look round. The site itself was once made up of small units that all mirrored themselves. Each of the unit had a front doorway and a full-length roller blind shutter alongside where deliveries and the firm's vehicles could be put and locked up securely at night time. By now however, the inevitable hoard of vandals had made their mark on virtually everyone of the premises. All but a few shutters had been broken open and most of the windows in the units had been smashed just for fun. Dave was just about to do an about turn as he neared the dead end on one of the side roads, when something caught his eye. He Approached the end of the dusty and rock strewn roadway with caution, turning his head from side to side making sure that he wasn't being observed. Once at the end of the road, he stood to one side and looked at the ground with interest.

"Sir," called Sam as he approached where Dave was standing. "I've put that request in for the traffic stop and question and they told me that it would be put in operation today as soon as possible."

"Ok," replied Dave still looking down at the roadway. "Come here Sam and tell me what you see?"

Sam walked towards where Dave was standing and was immediately gestured to one side by Dave's hand waving.

"What have you found?" asked Sam.

"You tell me?" replied Dave still looking down at the roadway.

Sam then followed Dave's gaze and soon picked upon a set of tyre tracks embedded in the layer of sand and dust that had built up over a long time. "These are tyre tracks and that look as though they came from a heavy lorry."

"Yes I know," said Dave. "But what's strange about them?"

Sam looked closer and after a while replied, "I can't see anything strange; they just look like tyre tracks to me!"

"Then look again," said Dave in a stronger tone of voice.

Sam did as he was told and restudied the tracks, then as if he'd been hit by lightening he called out, "They only go for a few feet and then they just disappear."

"Yes, they do," replied Dave nodding his head. "But more importantly, they all stop in a dead line as if they had been wiped out for some unknown reason!"

"Do you think that these tracks could have any bearing on this case sir?" asked Sam.

"Maybe, or then again maybe not, only time will tell us that. But for now, I want the forensic team to make copies of them before the rain comes and they get washed away," said Dave, as he walked along the roadway between the units towards the main road, looking for any more signs of the tyre tracks. "Look here Sam," said Dave as he bent down and pointed to a single tyre track in the sand. "I know this is only a single tread whereas the others were from a double wheeled axle. But the tread on the tyre looks very much the same to me, how about you?"

Sam stooped down to scrutinize the tread marks and replied, "They could be the same, but only the forensic boys will be able to confirm that I'm afraid."

"Well that's obvious, but for now, let's work on the theory that these tracks are somehow involved with our missing van, shall we. Why would they need such a heavy lorry in the first place and if they did use it, where the hell have they taken it and what's happened to the three men that were inside it and why haven't they been located yet?"

"It's the last part of that statement that concerns me sir," said Sam looking all around the area. "Why have they decided to keep hold of the men, I mean to say, kidnapping is not normally part of armoured van raids in this country, that God!"

"If it were a kidnapping, then it would mean that the men were all still alive and the onus for the ransom would be between the firm and their insurance company. What worries me is that it's a day on from the actual raid and there has been no contact from any potential kidnappers. I would have thought that the last thing they would want to do, is to keep three men locked up and away from their obviously fretful families, for a second longer than they had to. Then there is the money side of all this. Tell me, if you had just hijacked a van that had £300,000 inside it, would you fuck about trying to get even more out of a company for the return of its personnel?" said Dave scratching his head.

"Huh, not likely, I'd been well and truly gone as far away from this place as fast as I could," replied Sam smiling at that thought.

"Me too, and that what makes me believe that the driver and the crew didn't take the money, in fact I have a horrible idea that they are lying dead somewhere. Why or for what reason, they had to be killed I have no idea. But we have always found either the van or its crew well before this length of time. The money is only a by product of the crime in my eyes, finding out who did it and stopping them has always been my top priority," said Dave as Sam's mobile phone rang out breaking the mood.

"Hello, yes that's right, oh that could be interesting, could you text me the firm's address and we'll take it from there? By!" said Sam as he ended the call.

"Good news I hope!" said Dave.

"Could something or nothing, depending on the way you look at it?" replied Sam.

"Jesus, do you always have to use ten words when a couple would do!" said Dave with a sigh in his voice.

"Sorry sir," replied Sam sheepishly. "That was the police control room. They told me about a report they've just received, from a company about one of the lorries being taken away for a few hours from their premises and then it was found again a few miles away intact!"

"A flatbed?" asked Dave.

"No, one of those bloody great lorry cranes, who, on earth would want to steal one of those things and hope to get away with it?" said Sam.

"Ah but in fact, they did get away with it, didn't they. If you saw one of those great lumbering things out on the road, would you think that it had been stolen, no you wouldn't. You'd probably think that you'd like to have a go driving it though wouldn't you, eh!" said Dave with a smile on his face. "Did they have any idea how far the crane had travelled since it was stolen?"

Sam looked again at his text message from the control room and replied, "Under, forty miles then reckon it had been driven."

"And how far is that particular firm and the place that the lorry was recovered, from this place?" asked Dave, hoping that Sam could work that sort of thing out quicker than he could.

"Well by my calculations, I make the round trip thirty six miles, give or take a mile or two," said Sam. "Do you think it's a coincidence?"

"No, coincidences are for people that can't find an alternative reason for something occurring at the same time. No, I believe that this crane for whatever reason, is somehow connected to this hijack, all we have to do now is to prove it!" said Dave. "Tell the forensic chaps about the crane and let's see if they can come up with anything. In the meantime, I think that we should have another look around this industrial estate and see if we've been missing anything else, shall we."

For the next hour, the two men walked around making entry to as many of the units that was possible for a quick shufty around inside. Then along the back row of old units, they discovered three that had their roofs destroyed. Not by fire, as is the usual type of vandalism, but smashed in with what looked like something heavy from above. Then the debris had all been moved to one side. From the outside of the units, the roof sections all looked as though they were still in place. Was this one of those coincidences again or had there been a party inside and the centre had been cleared for the dancing and drinking to go ahead?

"Hey sir, come and take a look at this?" said Sam as he gestured to Dave to come.

Dave made his way across the dirt-covered floor to where Sam was standing.

"What have you found?" asked Dave as he neared Sam.

"Well the back wall of this unit appears to have been knocked down and outside there is what looks like a relatively fresh huge mound of dirt," said Sam as he pointed out the pile to Dave.

"Yes I can see it," replied Dave. "It looks as though it's been dumped there by fly tippers after doing a job to save them money."

"Oh, I thought that I'd found something," replied Sam sounding a little dejected. "But with hindsight, we haven't found any holes in the ground that all that dirt could have come out of have we?"

"Well, not yet we haven't," smiled Dave. "But the day's still young though isn't it! Come on, let's go and have a chat with some of the missing men's families. Maybe they will be able to shed some light onto their disappearances, who knows!"

4

Outside the semi detached home of William Brown, who is one of the drivers that have gone missing. The two detectives took a moment before they went to interview his wife, to get a feeling for the area. As they looked up and down the street, they would have been hard pressed to pick out his address from all the other houses without first knowing its number. It appeared that every pair of semi-detached properties is a mirror image of the one next door.

Walking up the front path they were met by, what looked like, a three hundred pound female in her fifties with a square shaped chin that looked as though it was made of granite.

"Wadder you pair want?" demanded the robustly built woman who stepped in front of the two detectives, preventing them from advancing any further along the path.

"We are police officers and we have come to have a word with a Mrs Brown, would that be you by any chance?" said Dave taking out his warrant card and showing it to her, secretly hoping that it wasn't.

"No, I'm Beth's next door neighbour Mary, I've been stopping those bloody reporters from constantly knocking on her door," she replied after looking closely at both their ID's before answering. "Have you found the cheating bastard yet, if so, then tell him that I'd like to have a word or two in his ear when he comes back."

"No we haven't been able to locate her husband yet," replied Sam, standing well back from the woman.

"Huh, ok then if you follow me, I'll take through to meet her," said Mary, as she slowly turned her great body mass around and made her way up the path towards the front door.

Dave and Sam dutifully followed the female guard at a respectful distance. Her gyrating rolls of flesh were like watching a giant walrus trying to move gracefully on dry land, not very pretty. A fleeting glance was the only interaction that flashed between the two detectives and briefly drew a raised eyebrow or two.

Inside the eerily quiet house, the two detectives were shown into the front room and asked to sit down which they promptly did. Then seconds later, the slight frame of a female dressed in jeans and sweatshirt entered the room and stood facing Dave and Sam obviously in a very distressed state. Behind her in complete contrast still standing guard was her neighbour Mary complete with her granite chin. Dave and Sam immediately stood up and Dave said, "Mrs Elizabeth brown I presume?"

The female nodded without actually answering. Eventually she asked, "Who are you?"

"I am Detective Chief Inspector Geraint and this is Detective Constable Parsons, we have come here to ask you some questions about the disappearance of your husband William."

"Ted, I always called him Ted and everyone calls me Beth," she replied as if on automatic mode.

"Why don't you and your neighbour have a seat and then we can have a chat about you and Ted," said Dave, gesturing her towards a seat.

"But what about those bloody reporters?" spouted out the neighbour not wanting to leave her post?

"Oh don't you worry about them," replied Dave with a smile. "If they come back while we are here, then I'm sure DC Parsons here, will happily have a quiet word in their ear, ok!"

Beth gave Dave a half smile as she settled down on a chair facing the two detectives. "Have you found him yet my daughter Deana keep asking where he is? She's only six, what do I tell her?" she suddenly asked Dave.

"No, I'm sorry, we still have no idea what has happened to the men or the security vehicle they were all in?" replied Dave watching her every move and gesture.

"I told you, he's probably run off with that tart he's been seeing behind your back dear," said Mary interrupting Dave questioning.

"And why would you think that then?" asked Sam changing the tack of questioning.

"He's been seen with her by a couple of the women that live around here, but Beth here refuses to believe it, don't you dear," said Mary as she looked directly at her friend with her arms folded under her breast.

"He's not having an affair; he's told me that she's someone from work, that's all," replied Beth trying hard to defend her missing husband.

"Do you know the woman's name?" asked Sam, hoping for a lead in the case.

"No, I've never actually seen her with Ted and he's never told me about her," replied Beth with her head hung down.

"Would either of you have any idea if anyone had a grudge against Ted or any of the other missing men from his company?" asked Dave.

The two women shook their heads expressing their despair at the lack of useful information, purely by their physical actions. With that final question, Dave thanked Beth for seeing them and told her that he would be in contact as soon as he had any information with regards to the whereabouts of her missing husband.

Outside and while standing by the police car, Dave looked across the roof of the car and said, "Well what do you think about that snippet of information?"

"I think her Ted has trouble keeping it in his pants, that's what I think. I wonder who the other female was?" said Sam with raised eyebrows.

"Well I wonder what we will uncover at the next port of call, the Sterling residence," said Dave as they both climbed into the car and headed off.

———

5

Ten minutes later, they pulled up outside the home of Thomas Sterling, who was one of the other missing drivers. This was one of four terraced properties that looked as though they'd been built over a hundred years ago. The dark grey rugged walls, gave the appearance of being built out of a mixture of stone and brick that stretched up to meet with the old slate roof, that had a slightly wobbly looking chimney perched on the top. The front garden although not very wide was unusually long and partly turned over to growing vegetables down the one side. The front gate to the property in total contrast was broken and leaning against the posts that once supported it. As the two men walked along the uneven crazy paved path, each wondered what lay behind the closed front door and whether whoever was inside would be able to shed some light on the mystery. Sam, after getting the nod from Dave, pressed the doorbell and then stood back. From inside the property the sound of children calling out to their mom could clearly be heard then, seconds later, the door opened slightly and the face of a young boy looked out at them.

"Mom said to ask you what d'you want?"

This reaction brought a smile to Dave's face, remembering the times when his mom had sent him to the front door. "We are from the police, is your mom in?" asked Dave in a soft voice.

The front slammed shut and they could hear the young lad shouting, "Mom, it's the police outside and they want to speak to you!"

There was a brief pause in activity, then finally the door opened up and a woman in her mid thirties stood there holding the hand of a much younger girl.

"Yes, can I help you," said the woman politely.

"I wonder are you Mrs Christine Sterling?" said Dave in response.

"Yes, have you any news about my missing husband?"

"I am SDCI Geraint and this here is DC Parsons from Scotland Yard. I wonder if we might come inside away from prying eyes and ears?" said Dave.

"Oh yes, sorry," said Mrs Sterling standing to one side and allowing the two detectives to enter.

She then showed them into the lounge and asked them to sit down. The room was cosy with a three piece suit along with a television and the usual games consoles for the children. On the walls were framed pictures of the children from when they had been on holiday. Some of them were of them on a sandy beach with their dad while others were from when they had been sightseeing.

Mrs Sterling then called to her son and told him to take his sister out the back garden and keep her company, while she talked to the police officers. Begrudgingly he took a hold of the little girls hand and disappeared out of the room.

"I take it that these are your children," said Dave with a smile.

"Yes, and please call me Chris, whenever I'm called Christine it usually means that I've done something wrong, well that's how it was when I was a growing up. Anyway, Royston is ten and Clarissa is only five. They can sometimes be a handful when they are together but then on another day they can play quite happily. Now I take it that you are here about Tom and the other missing men?"

"Yes Chris, we want to get a picture so to speak of them and see if there is any reason for them to disappear other than, and I'm sorry to have to say this so bluntly, being hijacked!" said Dave.

"Well what can I tell you, Tom has worked for the company for about eight years? He's a good husband and provider and a loving father to the children. I really don't know what else I can tell you?" said Chris sitting back in her chair looking straight at the two detectives.

"Look, we have to ask everyone concerned these types of questions," said Dave. "To your knowledge, has he ever had an affair or just gone off without telling you before?"

"Huh, an affair, Tom, no way. For one thing, the job he does, doesn't pay that much, meaning that he has to do a lot of overtime whenever it becomes available. The only time he goes off on his own is to go fishing for a few hours but he always tells me where to find him if I need him."

"Do you ever meet up with any of the other men and their families?" asked Sam hoping to change the direction of questions.

"Oh we have all met up occasionally if one of them has a BBQ and invites us all round. That though only happens on rare occasions and it is always on a Sunday as that's the only day they all have off together, why do you want to know that?" asked Chris sitting forward on her chair and looking at Sam curiously.

"Oh it was just something that was mentioned by another lady about one of the drivers having a secret assignation with another woman and I wondered if you'd heard about it, that's all," replied Sam.

Chris sat back in her chair and smiled broadly, "Oh you've been talking to Beth's neighbour Mary haven't you. She's what commonly known as a, excuse my language, shit stirrer. Yes he has been seen several times with another woman in his car by me and his wife. It was only after she asked him about the woman did he realise how things could have become misconstrued. You see, the woman seen with him was the firm's secretary Fiona. I think her full name is Fiona Bliss. She's a pretty little thing and only works, I think three days a week and he used to give her a lift home if their shifts coincided, that's all. But when he realised people's perception to his, shall we say naivety, he stopped doing it."

"So you have no idea if anyone held a grudge against your husband or any of his workmates?" said Dave.

Chris thought hard for a second then replied shaking her head, "Nope, nothing like that comes to mind at all, sorry. Tell me something, do you believe that something terrible has happened to them?" This time her voice began to shake and Dave could visibly see her hands begin to tremble at that thought.

"To be honest with you Chris," said Dave looking straight into her eyes. "At this moment in time, we have no idea what has become of either the men or the vehicle they were travelling in. So until one or the other turns up, we at the Yard are working on the theory that they are all still alive and well. That is why we have to ask such personal questions, hoping to discover the real reasons behind their disappearance."

With that, Dave and Sam both stood up and thanked Chris for her time and told her that they would keep her informed if and when they find out something definite about her husband. Chris walked the two men to the front door and as she began to open it, she suddenly stopped and said,

"Look, I don't know if this is of any help to you, but there is a whisper going around that one of the drivers was having a fling with the wife of someone that also worked at the company. I don't know any names but it came to my ears through so called Chinese whispers. However, what I can tell you for sure is that my Tom is not the man you are looking for!"

Dave thanked her for seeing them and after shaking her hand, he and Sam headed back to their car.

"Bloody hell, it's like one of those soap operas," said Sam shaking his head in disbelief. "I mean to say, we've only been to two of the homes and we've already been told about two possible affairs, how many more will we find out about do you think?"

"Personally if people at this company want to have affairs, then that's down to them, all I'm interested in, is if one of the affairs provoked someone to hijack this van along with the men inside. Now if that turns out to be the motive behind all this, then the fate of all those men could have already been sealed!" said Dave opening up the car door.

"So do you think they are all dead then?" asked Sam in a more sombre tone of voice.

"I'm afraid only time will tell us the answer to that question but what concerns me is the fact that neither the men nor the van have been sighted yet. Why?" replied Dave climbing into the car. "I think we need to be informed about anything out of the ordinary, until this case is solved. Sam, let the control room know to pass that type of information past us first, so that we can decide if it is useful or not, will you."

6

While driving back to the Yard, Dave suddenly asked Sam, "Wouldn't someone have to have a HGV licence, or at least have experience in driving large vehicles, to be able to drive something as cumbersome as that lorry crane without creating mayhem?"

"I would think so," replied Sam. "I'd think the average bloke wouldn't have a clue how to drive something like that. I mean it must be one of those childhood wishes but not something most of us would ever get the chance to fore fill."

"I wonder if any other large vehicles have been stolen or like the crane, borrowed recently," said Dave, his mind now stepping up a few gears. "Maybe that's how the security van along with the men was hijacked. If they couldn't get into it and drive it away the van, for whatever reasoning behind that was. Could it be a possibility that the crane had been used to somehow lift the van wholesale onto the back of a lorry and then covered up while they stole it away? But the one thing that still niggles me, why bother with all that messing about, when they could have just blown the doors of the back of the van and taken the money. Surely, that would have easier for them to do and with much less fuss. I don't know, I'm getting a bad feeling about this robbery, everything we've found out so far has told us absolutely nothing. We are either missing something vital, or looking at the whole caper the wrong way but for the life of me at the moment nothing seems to be panning out."

Back in their office at the Yard, while Sam went and got some fresh mugs of hot coffee from the machine, Dave got down to the boring chore of going through his in tray paperwork. Most of the papers just needed his signature as the y senior officer in the office. One scrap of paper however caught Dave's eye. On it was a scribbled note about a complaint from some anglers. They had called the police to tell them that someone must have driven a car into a disused quarry were they fished and the fuel and oil was leaking out and killing the fish stock. Dave was just finishing reading the note as Sam returned with the mugs of coffee.

"What do you think of this?" said Dave handing the note across to Sam.

Sam read it carefully and then tossed it back onto the desk and said, "It's probably joy riders dumping the car in the water to hide it, after they'd nicked and drove about in it for a while."

"Mm, you're probably right," replied Dave as he took a long slurp of his coffee. Then he suddenly fell silent and went into deep thought!

Then without saying a word to Sam, he reached over and picket up the phone and called the control room. "Hello Sgt, DCI Geraint here. I've just read a note that was left on my desk about some anglers and a vehicle being dumped in the old quarry. I want you to arrange for the police divers to attend the quarry to ascertain if it is a car in there or something else. What, oh yes, I want this put down as a high priority, thank you!"

"What was all that about?" asked Sam leaning forward on the desk. "I told you it's probably an old banger that's been dumped after being trashed by kids, that's all!"

"Mm, you're probably right but what if it's the missing security van in there and that's the reason we've not been able to find it?" replied Dave feeling a little more upbeat about things. "Anyway, if you're right then the underwater search team will be getting a free practice dive out of it at least and we might even be able to save some of the fish by retrieving the vehicle out of the water!"

"You love working on hunches don't you," said Sam taking another long drink of his coffee.

"Hey, what's the point of having the bird shit on your shoulder if you can't pull a few strings occasionally!" replied Dave smiling broadly.

It was a couple of hours later when Dave got a phone call about the vehicle found in the quarry. After replacing the receiver, he looked at Sam and said, "Well, we were both wrong, that was the lead diver from the search team up at the quarry. He's just been told that the vehicle they've discovered is not a car or our missing security van but a flatbed lorry used to carry those big sea going containers. It looks as though for some reason, it's somehow been driven into the quarry minus any container and ended up lying on a ledge over twenty metres down."

"Could the container have just come of the back and dropped to the bottom?" asked Sam.

"I asked the team leader that same question and he assures me that they have had divers looking along the bottom and there is no sign of any container. They are now arranging for the lorry to be dragged out and will get back to us as soon as they have anymore news," said Dave.

"So we found large tyre tracks at that old abandoned industrial estate, a mobile crane was borrowed and then returned. Now we have a flatbed lorry discovered in an old quarry, are they all connected in our crime or are they just in the picture to somehow distract us?" said Sam.

"Right now I'm just concentrating on the case in hand, especially as the quarry is on the very same road as the hijack took place!" said Dave. "Sam, what I want you to do, is to put the names of everyone concerned with that security firm into the computer and find out if any of them has or has ever held a HGV licence. There far too many friggin stolen lorries involved in close proximity to this crime for my liking!"

7

It was the following morning before the dumped lorry could be extradited from the quarry and the forensic people from the Yard able to inspect it. The list of people submitted by Sam for cross checking with those that had HGV licences were also now available for Dave and Sam to evaluate.

"Morning sir," said Sam as Dave entered the office.

"Morning Sam, is there any helpful news yet?"

"Well, according to records at the DVLA, none of the people at the security firm hold or have ever held a HGV licence. So we're no further forward on that tack then," replied Sam. "Coffee?"

"Mmm, yes please," replied Dave sitting at his desk. "I don't know about you but this case is puzzling and everything was going around in my head all last night."

"I was thinking about that and I was wondering, if these lorries are connected with this case, then the area for th hijacking is quite restricted. I mean if they did use the crane to load it onto the flatbed and both of them are still within a small area, then surely so must the men and their vehicle be around here too!" said Sam.

"Yes, that's the same line of thought that I've been thinking," replied Dave. "The only fly in the ointment is the fact that the crane never went far from where it was taken from, then to the old industrial estate and back to where it was recovered. So if that is true, then how the hell did they get the van off the flatbed once it reached its final destination?"

"Ah, I never thought of that part of the puzzle," replied Sam a little sheepishly.

"Well if we could all think of everything, then half of us would be out of a job wouldn't we?" replied Dave, taking his first long slurp of his early morning coffee. "I think we should go back to the estate and have another good look around. This time though, we'll have to try and get inside everyone of those old and battered units."

"Does that mean forcible entry?" asked Sam sounding like a little boy, being let loose.

"Officially no, however if there happens to be a broken window or two which allows us access to the unit, then that will be acceptable. Do I make myself clear?" said Dave.

"As mud sir," replied Sam smugly.

As soon as they had finished their coffee, the pair made their way down to the rear of Scotland Yard where the unmarked police cars are parked.

"You drive this time," said Dave as he tossed the keys across the roof of the car.

As they were driving across to the old industrial estate, Dave's mobile rang out.

"Hello, yes that's me. Oh that's interesting, ok let me have your report a.s.a.p." said Dave as he ended the call.

"Who was that?" asked Sam while concentrating on his driving.

"That was Stu from forensics, he's just given the lorry from the quarry the once over. What he has told me is that the lorry had been driven into the quarry as it was still in gear when it was retrieved. Also, the locks used to hold a container were all in the open position meaning that if there had been a container loaded on it. Then it had already been removed prior to the lorry entering the water," said Dave.

"So your theory that the van and the men must still be in this area is looking more and more realistic," said Sam as they neared the old industrial estate.

Pulling up at the entrance, Sam parked the car and they both got out. I don't know, there's a lot of old units on this site to search thoroughly with just the two of us sir," said Sam.

Dave looked around and finally nodded his head and replied, "Yes, you're right Sam. Tell you what; do we have such a thing as a cadaver dog or a dog that can detect dead bodies?"

"I'll get onto control and ask them to find out for us. If they have one then I will get them to send a unit out to us here," said Sam.

So while he got on with that, Dave began his look into some of the nearby units. Sam caught him up a few minutes later and told him that a dog unit that specialised in finding dead bodies would be with them shortly. In the meantime the dog handler asked if we could stay out of the buildings that he had to search so that there was no cross contamination from one unit to another.

Dave nodded his head and reluctantly withdrew with Sam back to the car to await the dog handler's arrival.

"So you believe they are dead, don't you sir. Otherwise you wouldn't have requested such a specialised dog unit!" said Sam.

"To be honest, I don't have any thoughts either way. However, if the dog comes up empty on this site then it helps to eliminate a huge search area and gives us more reason to think more positive doesn't it!" replied Dave.

It was just under an hour later when the dog unit finally arrived and to Dave's surprise there wasn't one unit, there was two!

"DCI Geraint I presume," said the dog handler. "Is there any particular part of this site that you want us to concentrate on?"

Dave gave the handler a quick nod and replied, "No, I need the entire site checking out. If there are any bodies hidden here, then there will be the three men from the security van heist the other day."

"Ok sir, if you two would wait here by the car while we begin our search, then we will call you if we find something," said the handler as the two dog units entered the site. With one of the units going to the furthest end of the site, while the other began his search close to the two detectives.

"God I hate this part of the job," said Dave as he began to pace up and down.

"I know sir, like you, I would prefer to be up the sharp end and know what's going on," replied Sam who was also itching to go. "But as you said earlier, the dogs can cover this place much quicker than we could and we could miss what they wouldn't!"

Two long hours later, the police radio crackled into life, "DCI Geraint, can you come to the second road on your left, we think we've found something."

Before the message had ended both Dave and Sam were on the move. At the second road on their left, they could see the two dog units waving for them to come to them. Half walking, and half running, they both hurried to the unit concerned.

"Sir, the dogs gave no indications on any of the other units. However, inside this one they both gave strong signs that there are bodies inside."

"Will you show me where exactly they think the bodies are?" said Dave.

Walking into the unit, the dog handler aloud the dog to show where he thought the bodies were hidden. As the men watched, the dog's nose sniffed the ground, made its way to the centre of the floor area and then sat down.

"There you are sir, it appears that there are bodies buried below the unit's floor!" said the dog handler.

"Sir, isn't this the same unit we were in the other day that had a huge pile of dirt stashed behind the rear of the unit," said Sam as he hurried to the rear of the unit and looked outside. "Yes it is, but the floors in these places are concrete aren't they?" said Sam looking confused.

Dave, after hearing Sam picked up a piece of metal that had been lying on the ground and proceeded to scrape at the floor. To everyone's surprise, as he thrust the metal bar into the floor, they soon discovered that it was not made of concrete like all the others but was compacted dirt.

"We need to have this whole floor dug up and quickly," said Dave taking out his mobile phone.

He then told the control room where he was and what he needed to get the job done. Then after thanking the two dog units for their input and releasing them to other duties. They had to play the waiting game once more, until help arrived.

8

As more police officers began to arrive, a plan of action was quickly drawn up. By now it was getting late in the day and Dave knew that no matter what happens, answers to what is buried beneath the floor of that unit must be answered before anyone was going home.

A JCB digger arrived soon after to commence with the initial heavy work. Powerful ARC lights arrived later and were quickly positioned, around the outside of the unit, to allow plenty of light for the officers inside to work by. Initially, the JCB was put to work inside the unit carefully scraping the top surface of the floor away. Then it was down to the manual work of the police officers using spades and other implements, to remove the soil bit by bit. This was not only painstakingly slow but also very arduous for the men doing it.

As this investigatory dig looked like it was going to take all night. Dave took the initiative and made arrangements for a mobile cafeteria to take up position away from the main roadway but close enough to the dig for the men to get some refreshments. The unit next to where they were digging, was opened up after gaining access through a broken window. Then after some ingenuity by a couple of officers, the toilets were made usable once more, to the great relief of most of the people there. After almost four hours of digging, one of the officers suddenly called out, "Sir, I've found something!"

Immediately, everyone stopped what they were doing and made their way across to the officer to see what he had found.

"What have you found?" asked Dave as he looked down into the hole where the officer was standing.

The man didn't reply, he just raised his spade in the air and then thrust it down into the soil by his feet.

Clang!

"It sounds like you've hit something metal," said Sam jumping down the few feet into the hole. Then using another spade he began to scrape away the soil until something red began to appear beneath him. Then using the head of the spade he tapped down on it once more.

Once again, there was a clanging sound, "Sir it looks to me like this is a container or something like that," said Sam.

"Ok, I want everyone out of the hole," said Dave. Then he turned to the JCB driver and asked, "If we clear what metal we can from around the edge of the hole. Do you think you could use you machine to clear the top of whatever is down there for me?"

"Yes, oh what is your name?"

"Paul Smith,"

"Well as long as you sanction it and if I do any damage to whatever is down there, you ensure that I won't get into any trouble!"

Dave smiled and replied, "Look Paul, if you want, I'll even give you a written note for your boss, ok!"

"Ok!"

So as soon as the area around the hole was as clear as they could make it, Paul the JCB driver re-entered the unit through the rear doorway and began removing the top surface of soil covering the metal object from the extremities of the hole. Now with the powerful jaws of the big digger making mincemeat of the soil beneath it, it wasn't long before he had managed to clear the top of the container. Now with the digger outside the unit, Dave and Sam for the first time had the opportunity to see just how big it was.

"Jesus, that's a big bugger," said Sam as he looked from one end of the container to the other. "What would you sat it is, thirty foot long!"

"It would look about that long," replied Dave shaking his head from side to side.

"What I want to know is why has it been buried here and by who?" said Sam who was almost mesmerised by the find.

"Mm, the thing that concerns me is what's inside it that warranted it being buried in the first place?" said Dave. "Now we have to think of a way of getting it back out again!"

"Well what about that mobile crane company, you know, the one that had a crane borrowed the other day!" Sam had just finished speaking when the reality of what he had said suddenly struck him. "Oh shit, you don't think that was why the crane was taken do you?"

"Could be," replied Dave. "So let's get hold of another mobile crane shall we. Maybe someone from outside the area so that we don't manage to cross contaminate the area."

"I don't think we'll get one here before tomorrow," said Sam. "Is that ok?"

"Yes that'll be just fine. Arrange for a heavy police guard on this place overnight though and I don't mean using any of these chaps after they've been doing the digging for the past few hours either," said Dave as he went and thanked Paul for all his help. "You do understand that you cannot reveal anything about what has been found here to anyone, not even your wife!"

"Yeh, the wife will think I've been down the pub all night anyway. Oh by the way, will you want me back here again tomorrow just in case there's some more digging out to do?"

"Why not," said Dave. "We'll see you here around eight o'clock, ok!"

"Wicked, then if it ok with you, I'll leave my digger here and cadge a lift back with the mobile cafe man," said Paul.

Dave gave him the nod and off he disappeared into the darkness. So with all the arrangements in place for the police officers that had been doing all the digging to be taken back to the Yard and the relief officers to be on guard duty.

A now very weary Dave and Sam climbed into their car and headed off back to the Yard and then home.

The night though didn't bring Dave much rest, he now had even more questions than answers. What would they find inside the container tomorrow, the missing van and the crew, or could it be that the container was actually nothing to do with his case. However, the one question that remained was, why would anyone go to all the trouble of burying such a massive thing. The answer always came back to the same answer and that was that whoever had buried it never wanted its contents to see the light of day ever again!

It was as these questions were spinning around in his head that Dave finally drifted off into a deep sleep.

9

At seven o'clock Dave was being driven by Sam towards the crime scene. The topic of conversation was obviously about the find last night and what they would find hidden inside the container.

"Do you think the missing security van will be inside?" asked Sam. Who was sounding bright and refreshed?

"Part of me hopes that it is, yet there's a big part of me that doesn't. Because if the van is in there then are the men also in there as well?" replied Dave.

As they pulled off the main road and into the abandoned industrial estate they were confronted by a uniformed police officer. He stood in front of their vehicle preventing them from passing.

After they had both showed their warrant cards to the officer they were allowed to proceed. Ahead of them was a huge mobile crane which was already positioned next to the unit where the container was buried. Paul, the JCB digger driver was also waiting and was standing talking to the crane driver.

"Morning gentlemen," said Dave as he approached them. "I take it that you are the crane driver?"

"Yes sir, Bill, Bill Ward."

"Right then Bill let's go inside for another look at our little problem shall we?" replied Dave.

Then all four men entered the unit for a fresh look at what lay ahead of them. "Right as you can clearly see, we have found this container buried and we need to have it raised up out of the ground so we can see what's inside it. Tell me Bill, will your crane be able to lift that thing up or not?" asked Dave looking directly at the crane driver.

Bill then took his time and had a walk around the hole in the ground for a good look at what he was being asked to do before he answered Dave.

"Do you know how heavy it is?" asked the Bill.

"No, and we don't know if the containers full or empty," said Sam.

With that, Bill jumped down onto the top of the container and picked up a spade. Then as the others looked on, he raised the spade over his head and brought it down hard striking the metal top of the container with a great force. A dull sound emanated from within the container making Bill shake his head from side to side.

"Well I can tell you for sure this things not empty, in fact it sounds to me that it could be quite full," said Bill as Sam offered him a helping hand and helped him to climb out of the hole. "What do you believe could be in there? The, only reason for me asking is to try and access what amount of weight might the entire containers could be?"

"Well if I was to tell you that it could have inside a missing security vehicle, would that help?" said Dave who was by now feeling a little frustrated.

"Ok, I should be able to lift that, but I'll need help to attach chains to the four corners to allow me a lifting point," replied Bill.

"I'll do that," replied Paul, as he followed Bill back to the crane.

"Right Sam, we need to clear the area and give these chaps a wide berth," said Dave, as he watched the two men drag heavy-duty chains from the crane and into the unit. Then they took an end each and attached the chains to the lifting brackets situated on each corner. Then Bill climbed into the crane and started it up. A black plume of smoke, was projected into the air as the driver revved to engine and began to raise the jib of the crane into the air.

All eyes were transfixed on the enormous hook, as it was then lowered into the middle of the unit through the hole in the roof.

Dave and Sam watched from a safe distance as the digger driver gave expert directions to Bill using only hand gestures. When the hook was in position, Paul took it in turns, placing the rings on the ends of the chains onto the hook and locked them in place prior to beginning the lift. Bill then gave the thumbs up and the digger driver climbed out of the hole and watched from outside the unit through one of the broken windows. Then the cranes powerful engine began to rev up spurting out huge plumes of black smoke. As Bill began to lift the container the ground began to shake as if the ground didn't want to give up its secret. Time and time again the crane strained as it tried in vain to lift up the container, but even with its outriggers firmly planted on the ground allowing the crane a better purchase. The container just didn't want to move.

As the engine rev's dropped, Bill shouted to Dave, "It's stuck and if I use anymore pressure then I run the risk of tipping over!"

"I have an idea," shouted Paul as he jumped into his JCB and started it up. "As you try to lift it up, then I'll try giving the sides a tap with the bucket, ok!"

Bill gave Paul the thumbs up and waited for him to reposition his Digger alongside the container. Then with them both happy with the situation, Bill began revving up the cranes powerful engine. Then he attempted to raise the container but as before, it remained stuck. Then it was down to Paul, he stretched the arm of his JCB out and gave the side of the container a gentle tap.

Clang, as the metal bucket of the digger and the container met under extreme force. But although the contact reverberated along the container, it remained stuck. Then Bill rammed the bucket in between the dirt wall and the metal side and began to wiggle it about. While this was happening, Bill revved the cranes engine even higher and began to jolt the jib of the crane up and down. Then as the chains creaked and groaned as if they were about to break under the extreme strain, it suddenly began to lift up out of the hole. Paul quickly reversed the digger out of the way; as Bill slowly raised the container clear of the unit's roof section. Dave and Sam stood pressed hard against the wall of the unit making sure that they kept clear of the dirt and debris that was now falling off the container and showering the surrounding area.

Soon the huge container was safely on the ground and the two detectives had their first unobstructed look around it. "Take a note of the serial number written on the side in case we need it to trace where it originally came from," said Dave, as he took the time took have a good look all around the container.

"Well it looks like there is only a set of double doors on the one end of the container," said Sam. "Now that's strange, why would you bother to padlock a container when you're going to put it in the ground?"

Dave moved forward and sure enough, there in plain view was a high security padlock. "This is looking stranger by the minute," said Dave. "Will someone get hold of an angle grinder to cut this lock of?"

Minutes later the lock was lying in pieces on the floor allowing the metal doors to be opened. This was the part of his job that Dave always hated. Nevertheless, as he was not the type of leader, to order subordinates to do these unpleasant tasks for him. "Right, before anyone goes near the container, they must be wearing gloves so as not to contaminate the potential crime scene." Then he took a deep breath and took hold of one of the levers that secured the door, lifted up and swung it to the side. As the door seal broke, the air was filled with the unmistakeable sickly stench of death. Everyone covered their mouths and noses with hands and hankies as they prepared themselves for what they would find inside the dark container. Then, with the willing help of a couple of his officers, they managed to pull the heavy door open wide.

As the light of day shone down through the opening it revealed lying on the floor, was the unmistakeable corpse of a female. They could only distinguish that fact because the body was dressed in female clothing. Her dark hair was matted and stuck to the crinkled skin covering her terror stricken face. Her jumper was dirty from the inside of the container while her light grey trousers were soiled from the release of her bodily fluids at the point of her demise.

Behind her filling the entire width of the container, was the rear of the missing security vehicle, which was quickly identified by the vehicles own registration plate.

"Who the hell is the woman?" asked Sam as he stooped down closer to look at her shrivelled body.

"I've no idea," replied Dave. "I didn't even know that there was a missing female. One thing's for sure though is that she was not part of the crew in the van, they were all men. So how come she's been left in here?"

Dave then carefully entered the container, stepping over the body, he tried pulling on the rear doors of the van to see if they would open but they are well and truly locked or sealed from inside.

"How bizarre, it appears that the rear doors are still sealed. Does that mean that the money is still inside or what?" said Dave as he moved to look down the side of the vehicle. "Mm, now that's interesting, the door mirrors are both folded in and are wedged tight against the side of the container. If the two drivers were still inside the van when it was put in here, then they wouldn't have been able to get out of the van. That means that they are going to be still in the front, but by now they're both going to be dead. We must now retire from the crime scene and get Stu from forensics out here so he can begin to quickly get us some answers!"

It was almost an hour before Stuart Green the Yard's medical examiner and his team arrived at the crime scene. After the obligatory crime scene photos were taken to help complete the chain of evidence. Stu made a quick inspection of the female remains and told Dave that in his opinion, she had not died due to any blunt force trauma but of suffocation, probably from lack of oxygen when the container was sealed and then placed into the ground and covered up.

"Are you saying that she was alive when she was put inside that thing and buried?" said Sam.

"Almost certainly," replied Stu. "From my initial examination I can see no defence wounds or in fact any wounds at all. That's what brings me to the conclusion that she was put in here alive when the doors were shut."

"What kind of bastard would do that sort of thing to a woman?" said Sam, his emotions running higher than normal.

"A really pissed off and cold hearted person in my book," replied Stu. "And I would imagine that the culprit you should be looking for is a man."

"Why do you say that?" asked Sam, curiously.

"It's because of the weight of those bloody doors, if I'm not mistaken, eh doc?" said Dave, butting in. "You see, they'd be much too heavy for a female to close and lock with another female on the other side trying hard to stop her from killing her, that's why!"

"Exactly," said Stu standing up to allow other members of his team to remove the woman's body.

"Doc before we have this thing picked up again and transported back to your lab. I have to know if the men are still inside or not?" said Dave.

"Well from first impressions, the van appears to be wedged meaning that whoever was inside the rear of the van would have had no means of escape. The drivers on the other hand might have, oh hang on a mo, will you? Tom, I wonder, could you manage to squeeze under that van and take a quick look-see up at the front and tell me if the drivers are in the cab or not?"

Tom, who was by far the slimmest member of Stu's team, bent down and took a quick look beneath the van, then, gave Stu the thumbs up. Then just like a rat up a drainpipe, he lay down on his back and began to slide his slim body beneath the chassis of the van. A few minutes later, he reappeared and told Stu, "Unfortunately I could see two men still in the front of the cab and they both appear to be dead. However, I did find something that might interest you at the front of the container and that was a heavy duty winch."

"What the hell is a winch doing in there?" asked Dave.

"Well it looks as though it had been attached to the front of the van. Then it was probably remotely operated, resulting in the van being dragged inside and becoming wedged on both side, preventing either of the men inside from escaping," said Tom. "It looks like the poor bastards never stood a chance."

"I know, however, why didn't they try to escape? If that had been me or you, the thought of being locked inside that thing would have been a no brainer in my view. Either you died quickly trying to escape or die slowly inside that metal coffin, I know which option I would chose if I had to make it. What's the odds that when you eventually open the van up, the money will still be inside!" said Dave.

"Do you mean that this wasn't a hijack after all!" said Sam.

"Well we'll know the answer to that when we discover if the money is still there or not?" replied Dave. "However, I don't want any of this getting out to the press or back to the families until we can confirm the identities of the people who are inside, ok. Sam I want you to go and have a word with Bill and Paul the crane and digger drivers. And explain to them the importance of keeping a lid on what they've seen here today!"

So as Sam went off to have a word with the drivers, Stu turned to Dave and asked, "I wonder if you have any idea how we're going to transport this thing back to the Yard."

Dave gave him a nod and replied, "There's a flatbed truck already on its way. All that's required is the help of the crane driver to put it on the back of the lorry, then for him to do the reverse at the other end. I'll go and have a quiet word with him right now!"

———————

10

   It had been one hell of a day so far for Dave and Sam. Now after completing the reams of paperwork that always follows any murder case, it was finally time for them to relax and take stock of the day so far.

"Tell me Sam, how many women are we aware of that are in some way connected to Barnes Securities?" asked Dave, downing a welcome slurp of hot coffee.

"Erm, there's the Elizabeth Brown and Christine Sterling who are both the wives of the two drivers. Then there's a Sonya Conway, who's the wife of one of the control room staff. Finally, there's a Miss Fiona Bliss, who's the part time secretary at the company. There are obviously more but those are the only females that I am aware of concerning this particular case," said Sam putting down his notes.

"I think that we should try to make contact with all four of them under some unrelated pretext just to reassure that they are still alive. If we can ascertain that they are, then at least we will be able to cross them off our list as the body in the box!" said Dave. "Right, if you try to get hold of the secretary, I'll try the other two women."

"Hello, is that Mrs Brown, Elizabeth Brown. This is DCI Geraint, my colleague and I spoke to you the other day."

"Yes, I remember, have you any news of my husband yet?"

"No, not yet," replied Dave calmly. "I've been trying to get hold of Mrs Sterling but she doesn't seem to be answering the phone. I was wondering if you had any idea where she might be."

"Oh Christine, yes she told me that she and her two kids were going to stay with her mother for a while until you find out what's happened to our husbands. She's been fed up of the press constantly ringing her up or knocking on her door. I have a number for you to contact her if you really need to," replied Beth in a quiet voice. "Tell me honestly, do you believe that they are still alive?"

"Well the way I like to look at things is that until I know different, then I work on the fact that they are. That way the urgency to locate them doesn't diminish," replied Dave.

"You will let me know as soon as you have any news though won't you?" said Beth, her voice now beginning to shake.

"I promise, as soon as we know, then I'll let you and the other women know too, alright,"

With that, Beth hung up the phone and Dave sat back in his chair and let out a deep sigh. "Well, how did you get on?" said Dave to Sam as he finish his phone call.

"Well according to the company, our Miss Bliss has gone away on holiday with her boyfriend to somewhere in Spain, would you believe it!" replied Sam. "How about you?"

"Well I managed to speak in person to Beth Brown and she tells me that Christine Sterling has gone to stay with her mom and she's taken the kids with her to get away from the press," said Dave. "Now the only one left to make contact with is Sonya Conway, who's married to the chap who works in the control room. If you try her number, I'll get onto Stu and see if he's got any news for me."

So while Sam made his phone call to Sonya, Dave called his old friend Stu for and update.

"Stu, what have you got for me?" asked Dave.

"Well we've managed to cut the other end of the container off and removed the winch. By the way, I can confirm that it was a remotely controlled winch inside the container, because we've located the handset, it was found beneath the security vehicle. It must have been thrown inside just prior to the doors being closed. We're just cutting away the sides of the container to allow us access to the van doors. However, we will need the help of the security company to aid us to get the doors of the van open without damaging or losing any evidence from inside the vehicle itself. From looking into the front of the cab of the van, I can confirm that there are two males inside and they are both dead. They probably died from oxygen starvation just like the woman did. By the way, have you had any luck finding out who she was or what she was doing there?" said Stu as he paused for breath.

"To answer your first question about getting inside the van, I'll get onto the owner Mr Barnes and ask him to bring down a spare set of keys to you just in case his security van is found and access to the inside is urgently required. The other question with regards to the dead female, enquiries are still underway but as yet we have no clue as to who she is or why she was inside?" said Dave as he put down the phone.

Dave then waited for Sam to finish on the phone before asking, "How did you get on with contacting Mrs Conway?"

"Well I tried her home phone but got no reply, so I contacted her husband while he was at work and he told me that she had taken the children away for a short break while there's so much interest in the missing men by the reporters," said Sam. "But in my mind, he was too eager to tell me that."

"Did he happen to say where she'd taken them?" asked Dave.

"No,"

"Well we've got no reason to think he's telling us lies, in fact it's only what one of the other women have done, and for exactly the same reason," said Dave. "We really need to get a break in this case if we're going to solve it anytime soon."

11

Dave and Sam were both making their way down to autopsy after receiving a call from Stuart Green. On entry to the lab, they noticed that behind Stu, lying on the slab was the body of the dead female found inside the container.

"What have you got for me Stu?" asked Dave as the three men met.

"Well after doing a preliminary investigation on the female, my original diagnosis appears to be correct. She died from asphyxiation and not from any sort of other trauma," said Stu. "We've managed to get some fingerprints from her and ran them through the system but as of yet, we've had no hits come back."

"Were there any distinguishing marks on her body that could help us to identify who she is?" asked Dave hopeful of some positive feedback.

"Not that is visible, anyway," replied Stu.

"What about the men inside the van?" asked Sam?

"Unfortunately, I'm still waiting for the keys to arrive so we can open the doors without causing any damage or losing vital evidence in the process," said Stu.

Just then, a man entered the lab and handed a small package to Stu. "This was delivered to the front reception desk addressed to you," said the man.

Stuart signed for the package and proceeded to open it in front of Dave. "Bloody hell, it's the keys to the van," said Stu as he gestured for the men to follow him.

Down in the holding area below Stuart's lab, now housed the security van minus its metal shroud. All three men donned surgical gloves and stood behind Stuart as he tried the keys in the door locks. First he tried the driver's door but was unable to open it. Then he moved around to the passenger side and attempted to open the door. This time however, he was successful. As he carefully opened the door, once again the stench of death reached out and engulfed them. Inside the van Stuart could for the first time, see the bodies of the two men that had been trapped inside, when it was sealed inside the container. The horrific look of extreme terror etched on their faces, were a stark testament to the horror that they had gone through.

"Sorry Dave, I need to have the bodies removed by my colleagues to correspond with the chain of evidence. So unfortunately, I can't allow you or Sam to actually enter the front of the vehicle," said Stu as he edged backwards out of the doorway and carefully closed it behind him.

"Can we take a quick look in the back of the van?" asked Dave, not wanting to corrupt the crime scene for Stu. "I'm interested to see whether there is still someone in the rear and also if the van's internal safe is intact or not!"

Stuart went through the bunch of keys until he found one that would unlock the side door allowing them access to the inside. With great care, Stu slowly opened the side door. As before, the acidic stench of death began to burn the inside their nostrils, making Sam wrench.

"Look, if you're going to throw up, then do it over there!" said Stu pointing Sam towards the toilets.

Sam waved his hands back to him and managed to splutter, "No, I'll be ok!"

With the door open to its fullest, Stu grabbed hold of a torch and switched it on, to illuminate the inside of the vehicle. First Stu shone the torch towards the rear of the van where he discovered the dead body of a male, curled up leaning against the rear door.

"Well there is the third member of the van's crew!" said Stu with a deep sigh.

Dave leaned into the van just far enough for him to be witness to Stu's find. "Shine the torch on the van's safe Stu will you," said Dave moving out of Stu's way.

Stuart shone his torch from the body along the side of the van until he came across the internal safe. "Hear it is?"

"Is it intact or not?" asked Dave, who was itching to know the answer to that question.

Stu reached into the van, grabbed hold of the safes door handle, gave it a twist and a tug. "Well it appears to still be locked as far as I can tell from here," said Stu backing away from the door. "You'll have to wait until I'm able to get inside for a closer look before I can be positive of that though."

"Well it looks like it's time for us to go and inform, the now confirmed widows of these men, that we've finally found them," said Dave.

"Thanks Stu, let me know as soon as you find out anything of interest, no matter how small. We on the other hand, have some bad news to deliver," said Dave, as he and Sam made their way towards the stairs.

12

This was a day for all concerned, now the heavy weight of informing family members that their loved ones are gone forever officially has, once again finally arrived.

Outside the Brown residence where Dave knew Beth and her daughter were still waiting anxiously for news. Dave and Sam waited for the arrival of a WPC, prior to actually entering the home and delivering such devastating news. A couple of minutes later, the WPC arrived and Dave briefed her about what he was about to tell the widow and what her role would be after they had left.

At the front door, Sam rang the doorbell and then stood back. Seconds later Beth Brown appeared holding her daughter in her arms. As she looked into Dave's sad eyes, she knew that they had found Ted and the reality of the situation hit her like a bolt of lightning. She let out a loud scream and Dave grabbed hold of her and her daughter when he saw her legs begin to shake, prior to her passing out. So while Dave held onto Beth, Sam took hold of the little girl and handed her across to the WPC to look after. Then between them, they carried Beth's limp body away from the door, into her lounge and laid her down gently on the sofa. The little girl, when she saw the two men carrying her mom into the room, began to wail at the top of her young voice. She only quietened down when the WPC let go of her and she went and lay down next to her mom.

"Get an ambulance to attend, will you and tell them to make a silent approach so as not to upset the little girl?" said Dave to the WPC. While she did this, he turned to Sam and told him to go and have a look in the bathroom and see if there are any smelling salts in there.

For a few minutes, the room fell almost silent. The only sound came from the little girls muffled cries as she nestled her head tightly against her mother's chest for comfort. Minutes later, the paramedic arrived and along with his giant backpack, entered the house. Dave moved away from Beth and brought the paramedic up to date with the whole situation.

Sam then re-entered the room holding some smelling salts in his hand and offered them to Dave. "Give them to the expert he'll know how to use them much better than me!"

Beth shortly began to come round from her shock, initially she forgot what had happened and wondered why she was lying on the sofa with everyone standing next to her. Then her memory snapped back into reality and she began to cry and held on tightly to her daughter. Eventually, the paramedic was able to give her a check up and gave her the all clear; well as far as her health, issues were concerned. He advised her to get in touch with her doctor for something to help her sleep. Then he left and went on with his duties.

"Now Mrs Brown I know it's a stupid question but I need to ask, how are you feeling right now?" said Dave in a soft tone of voice.

"I'm alright," she replied, shuffling her legs from off the sofa, so as to allow her daughter to sit next to her. "So you've found him then!"

"Unfortunately, yes. We've found them all and the vehicle they were all in," said Dave looking straight at Beth.

"Where did you find him?" asked Beth with a shaky voice.

"Look all I can tell you at the moment is that they were all found together inside the van," replied Dave.

"But I need to know if he suffered or not?" said Beth, her once shaking voice was now turning to anger and it was being vented directly at Dave.

"Look, if you really want to know how and where we found your husband. Please allow the WPC here to take your daughter into another room so that she doesn't have to here the fine details, ok!" said Dave as he gestured to the WPC to take the little girl out of the room.

At first she didn't want to leave her mom, then Beth explained that the grownups needed to talk about her daddy. That was when reluctantly the little girl left the room holding onto the WPC's hand. As soon as the door to the room closed, Beth stared a Dave and asked how her Ted had died.

Dave took a deep breath and then explained how her husband and the others in the crew had all been trapped inside their van, put into a large metal container then they had all been buried underground.

"Were they alive or dead when they were buried?" asked Beth, the anger that had briefly been in her voice had now reverted to being shaky.

"Until I get the results from the autopsy's I'm afraid that I'm unable to answer that question for you," replied Dave.

Beth dropped her head into her hands and began to sob uncontrollable. The sound of Beth's crying however, was overheard by her daughter who came running into the room. When she saw her mom upset, she flung her tiny arms around her mom's neck and squeezed tightly.

"Don't cry mommy," said the little girl. "I'll look after you."

Those few words from such a little child brought more than a few tears to everyone that was inside the room.

Dave stood up and stood next to Beth and whispered, "This WPC will remain hear with you and assist you for as long as you need her, ok. When I have any more information for you then I will come and give it to you myself, all right. Now I'll have to go and tell the families of the other two men the bad news. Please don't talk to anyone before I've had the chance to speak to them personally. This is not the type of news you want hear especially over the phone is it. Oh by the way, can I have the address where I can get a hold of Mrs Sterling?"

Beth reached out for her address book and wrote down both the address and the phone number then handed it back to Dave. After giving Beth his condolence for the loss of her husband, he gave a nod to the WPC and he and Sam left the house and made their way back to their car.

"That poor family," said Dave with a deep sigh as he looked back towards the house. "What had they done to deserve this?"

"When we catch the bastard responsible for doing this, then I'll more than willingly be the one to ask that question," replied Sam, trying hard to compose himself.

Dave then took a look at the address of the parents of the other women they needed desperately to talk to. Beth had written it down for him, but only now had he realised that she was almost a hundred miles away from London.

The address was somewhere in Birmingham, which was much too far for him or any other officer to travel. Dave then took out his mobile and put a call through to the police liaison officer back at the Yard. He told him of the address and the name of the woman concerned. He then relayed his message that he wanted the local police liaison officer up in Birmingham to deliver. When he was sure that he had thought of everything that the woman needed to know, he ended the call.

"Well at least she will hear the devastating news first from an experienced police officer and not from a member of the press wanting to know how she's feeling right now!" said Dave almost spitting feathers at that last thought. "By the way, have we got an address for the parents of the other chap that died inside the van yet?"

"No, as far as I can find out, he has no close family still living," replied Sam as he desperately looked through his notes.

"Right then now that, that part of the job is out of the way. How about you and me, paying the security company another call, well at least we can tell them that we've found the van and the missing crew for starters!" said Dave as he climbed into the driver's side of the car. Then he started the car and sped off before Sam had a chance to put on his seat belt.

At Robert Barnes Securities Dave and Sam were shown by an employee directly into the owner's office, where Mr Barnes himself was sitting behind his large desk.

"Have you any news about the missing van yet?" asked Mr Barnes.

"As a matter of fact we have," replied Dave as he and Sam both pulled up a chair and sat down.

"Does this mean that you've found it then?" asked Mr Barnes getting all excited.

"Now isn't that interesting," said Dave, as he turned and looked towards Sam who was sitting alongside him. "Mr Barnes here has only asked if we've managed to find his van, not once has he asked if we've been able to locate the crew and if so how are they?"

"Do you think that could be because he already knows how they are?" replied Sam looking directly at Mr Barnes, who by now was looking very nervous.

"No of course I don't know how they are, how could I? I mean to say, they all went missing at the same time as the van, didn't they?" said Mr Barnes who was by now looking very uneasy and stumbling looking for the correct words to say next.

Dave then turned his focus back to the owner and said, "Yes, we've located you're van and yes, we've also located the three members of the crew. Unfortunately though, all of the three members of the crew are all dead!"

"Was the money still there or not?" asked Mr Barnes as he leant forward on his desk like a little boy looking for sweets to eat.

"Well shit, it's not hard to distinguish, where this heartless bastards priorities are, is it?" said Sam, who was itching to stand up and give the boss a piece of his mind.

Dave reached out and prevented Sam from rising off his chair. "Now hang on a minute DC Parsons, first things first. Mr Barnes, could you tell us if you were on duty in the office on the day that the van was hijacked?"

"What do you mean by that accusation?" spluttered out Mr Barnes as he stood up in protest, to the way he was being treated.

"It's a simple question, that only demands a simple answer," replied Dave in a calm manner.

Mr Barnes seemed to be taken aback by that question, so much that he sat down again as if he had to think about where he had been on that fateful day. "No, I was not in the office on that day. I decided to take the day off for some personal time, why do you want to know where I was."

"Can anyone vouch for your whereabouts on that day?" asked Sam joining in on the assault.

"Err, no I spent the day at home alone, why do I need an alibi for where I was?" asked Mr Barnes indignantly.

"Ah, well it appears that you are the only one that doesn't have a witness to vouch for your whereabouts, so I think that we should move this line of questioning down to Scotland Yard don't you DC Parsons?" said Dave, as they both stood up and moved towards Mr Barnes.

"I must protest, I'm innocent, you can't take me from here without arresting me, that's illegal, I know my rights!" shouted Mr Barnes as he refuse to get out of his chair for Sam.

"That suits me just fine," said Dave. "DC Parsons, will you arrest this man on suspicion of being involved with hijacking and four counts of murder."

"Murder, what are you talking about being responsible for murder, murder of who?"

demanded Mr Barnes, who was still refusing to get up out of his chair.

"Mr Robert Barnes, I am arresting you on suspicion of being involved with the hijacking of one of your security vehicles and being involved with the murder of four persons. "You do not have to say anything. But it may harm your defence if you do not mention when questioned something which you later rely on in court. Anything you do say may be given in evidence." Now I want you to stand up and place you hands behind your back for me," said Sam with a beaming smile across his face.

"I will not!" shouted Mr Barnes, standing his ground.

Dave then moved around the back of the desk and stood next to Sam. Then with a nod of his head, they both reached out and took hold of one of Mr Barnes wrists each and firmly applied wristlocks, until both of his hands were in a position behind his back enabling Sam to apply handcuffs.

"Sit him back down while I arrange for some transport for him back to the Yard," said Dave taking out his phone.

"But, your making a terrible mistake," said Mr Barnes but this time, his voice was almost quivering as he spoke. "I had nothing to do with hijacking or murder, like you've just accused me of!"

"Look, don't speak now, wait until your back at the Yard and you're solicitor is present if you say that you want one," said Sam putting his finger up to his own lips.

Twenty minutes later a marked police car pulled up outside the premise. Mr Barnes, still in handcuffs was escorted out of the building by police officers and placed in the rear of the car still protesting his innocence, then without hesitation, the police car drove off.

With him now out of the way, Dave and Sam made their way along the corridor to the control room. After gaining entry to the room after showing their ID's, they preceded to ask the two control room staff a few questions.

"Aren't you the two gents that were on duty the day that the van went missing?" said Dave as he approached the two men who were both sitting behind a bank of television screens.

"Yes, I'm Simon Hewitt and this is Peter Conway, why have you any news about what happened to them yet?"

Dave looked across at Sam and gave him the nod to take things from here. "Yes, we've found the van and the missing crew," said Sam stopping short of giving out too much information to the men in one hit.

"Are they ok?" asked Peter as he kept watch on the screens.

"Not really, you see they're all dead!" replied Sam as he watched the reactions of the two men.

"Dead, did you just say they're all dead, but why would they have to die just because of a robbery? It's the company policy that if they're ever confronted by would be robbers, then, they should hand over the money without trying to intervene but try to observe as much information as possible to help the police catch them at a later date," said Simon shaking his head in total disbelief. "They all knew that, so why did they all have to die?"

Just then, Dave's mobile phone rang out breaking the mood in the room. He moved to the far corner of the room and answered it. A few minutes later, he returned and said, "Well for your information, the money on the van is still there. Robbery could not therefore be the reason that those men died. The mood in the control room was now sombre to say the least.

"What does Mr Barnes have to say about all this?" asked Simon.

"Ah at the moment he isn't aware of that snippet of information. Instead, he's on his way at this moment to the Yard to, how should I put it, help us with our enquiries," said Sam with a slight titter in his voice.

"Now will you explain to me once again about how the people in the control room work the shift patterns?" asked Dave changing the topic of conversation.

Simon then stood up and took Dave over to where the control room staff who are on duty on any particular day, sign in and out at the beginning and at the end of their shifts.

"Have you ever known these actions to vary at any time?" asked Dave.

"What do you mean by that?" asked Peter from the other side of the room.

"Oh all I meant was that maybe from time to time, one of the team might need to leave early or even get in late and his team mate might cover, that's all," said Dave calmly.

"No well that sort of thing has never; happened in this place I can tell you that for nothing!" said Peter insistently.

"Ok, but it's only the type of questions that we as police officers have to ask, especially in a murder enquiry like this," replied Dave. "Oh by the way Peter, I can call you Peter can't I?"

"Yes, why do you ask?"

"Oh it's just that I tried to call your wife the other day and have a chat with her. You know the sort of thing I mean, did she know any of the other men or women that worked here and was she aware of any problems that they might be having, you know that sort of thing," said Dave casually. "But I haven't been able to get hold of her and I was wondering if you could tell me where she is, that's all?"

Peter stopped what he was doing and appeared to pause prior to him making any sort of reply. "Oh she's taken the kids away for a few days, she likes to try and get away especially before the schools break up and she says that it's a lot cheaper that way."

"When will she be getting back then?" asked Sam changing the direction of the questions.

"Oh it maybe a week, then again she could decide to stay a little longer, why all the concern with my wife?" asked Peter who was this time sounding a little more edgy.

"Well she's the only female connected to the firm and the dead men that we've not been able to speak too, that's all," replied Dave. "Maybe when she returns, you could tell her that's it's imperative that she gives me a call."

"Mm, maybe!" muttered Peter in response.

"I don't think you understand what I'm saying do you," said Dave who was by now becoming almost fixated on Peter's unusual reaction to his requests. "I would like you to give me an address or telephone number now, where your wife can be contacted, if not then I will have to take you down to the Yard for some further questioning, understand?"

Peter looked at Dave then glanced quickly towards Simon and then back to Dave. "Sam, will you get Simon to show you around outside the control room for a few minutes."

Sam looked momentarily a little confused at Dave, then realised that he needed to be alone with Peter and asked Simon to come outside with him for a while. As soon as the door closed behind them, Peter turned to Dave looked him straight in the eye and said, "Look, if you want the honest truth, Sonya has left me and taken the kids with her. She left the other day and for the life of me, I haven't got a clue where she or my two children are at the moment. However, I didn't want Simon or any of the others to know about that until they have to, alright?

"That's fine by me, you're private lives are your own business, however I will still need to have a word with her. Therefore, when she does get in touch with you, I would appreciate if you would tell her that from me," said Dave who at least understood Peter's lacklustre attitude.

Dave went to the door and told Sam that he could come back inside. As they passed, he whispered briefly what Peter had just told him and asked that he stays with him but keeps off the subject while he and Simon now went off for a chat. Dave closed the door behind him and he and Simon walked further along the small corridor until they came across an empty office. Once inside and away from inquisitive ears, Dave set about chatting to Simon trying to get him to open up about the workings of this place.

"Look Simon, I'm not really interested in what anyone in this company gets up to as long as it doesn't involve me. So why don't you tell me the truth about the goings on, especially in the control room and save me from fumbling about in the dark looking for all the answers," said Dave in a casual tone of voice.

"Look honest, I've told you the truth about how things work in there. I've even showed you the signing in and out book that proves it. So I really don't know what else you want me to say sir?" replied Simon.

"Ok then I'll tell you something shall I. You know those men that we all thought had been hijacked."

"Yes."

"Well that was just a ploy, for someone that I believe that either works in this company or used to work here, to murder one or all of those men. Do you know how they died, no, well then I'll tell you shall I. First of all they were forced while they were all still inside the van, into a huge metal container. Then the doors of the container were sealed up with them still trapped inside. To top it all, someone had somehow dug out a massive hole in the ground and the container along with its human contents were then placed into the hole and covered up!" said Dave, so if you know something, anything at all you must tell me now and stop fucking me and my officers about like you have been doing.

Simon lowered his head and then asked quietly, "Are you saying that they were all buried alive!"

"Yes, alive, imagine that happening to you, how would you feel if you knew that a work colleague was stopping the police from finding the culprit responsible for that heinous act. Just to cover up a breach of the rules that no one really give a rat's arse about, eh!" replied Dave as he lowered his aggressive mannerism.

"Look ok, we do sometimes fiddle the system," said Simon. "Occasionally one of us needs to either come in a little latter or leave a little earlier. On those occasions, we first of all have ensure that Mr Barnes will not be in the office on that day because he doesn't miss a trick if he's here. Then we just work the shift alone and because the door to the control room is always locked, the odds of being caught out are minimal to say the least."

"That's fine, now we both know that you both work the system to your own advantage. I'm not really concerned about that," said Dave. "However, what I am concerned about is whether you were both here on the day that the van went missing or not?"

"Look, I don't want to get anyone into trouble," said Simon who was obviously hesitant at spilling the beans on a fellow worker.

"If whoever was missing on that day and they've got an alibi for the time frame in question, then I'm not going to be interested. I'm only interested if they don't have one, meaning that they could be responsible for those men losing their lives, in the way they did?" said Dave.

"Well on that day, it was supposed to be Peter and me working the day shift. He told me that he needed some time off to try to reconcile his rocky marriage. He told me that his wife had told him that she was going to leave him and take his two kids with her. Well as I'm still single, I only thought it right that I should cover for him while he tries to save his marriage. I'm sure any chap would do the same if they were asked, don't you?"

"Tell me Simon, how long was Peter gone that day?" asked Dave, his questions now becoming more concise.

Simon thought for a while and then replied, "Oh yes, I remember now, he never actually came in that day and asked if I could scribble his name on the record book for him. When I asked if everything was ok, he just told me that they had left him and were not coming back and he needed some space to get his head around it all. So I did what he asked, and to be honest with you, we've never broached the subject again, well I mean you don't do you?"

"Ok now when we go back, I don't want you to say anything about our little chat to Peter otherwise he might think that you're, telling tales and possibly getting him into trouble with the boss, alright Simon," said Dave as he placed his hand on the door handle.

Simon nodded and the pair walked back into the room smiling as if nothing was wrong. "Ok, lads we must be getting back to the Yard as we've got your boss down there for questioning and he'll be getting a little upset with me if I keep him waiting any longer than needed," said Dave as he and Sam made their way through the open door.

13

Out in the car, Dave brought Sam up to date with his conversation with Simon.

"Do you think Peter had anything to do with these murders or not?" asked Sam as he climbed into the passenger seat.

"I don't know," replied Dave. "If only we could get in touch with his now estranged wife for confirmation of their split up and of course more importantly, to make sure that she and her kids are all ok!"

"Are we going to interview Barnes guv?" said Sam smiling. "I bet he's blowing a fuse by now."

"Yes we'll head back that way but there's no need to rush, the traffic around here is like trying to make your way through treacle isn't it?" said Dave.

"Mm, I see what you mean," replied Sam with a smile as he looked out through the windscreen of the car at a virtually empty road in front of them!"

It was over an hour later when the two men finally reached the interview room within the Yard. As they both entered the room, Mr Robert Barnes was already sitting at the table waiting for them.

"What's the meaning of keeping me here like this, I demand to see a solicitor immediately!" shouted Mr Barnes through clenched teeth.

"Oh haven't you already asked for a solicitor yet?" replied Dave as he moved closer to the table.

"No, I was waiting for you to arrive; I didn't think it would take this long though, did I?" said

Mr Barnes, his round shaped face by now beginning to turn a bright shade of red mostly through temper.

"Oh, well in that case we will have to wait until your solicitor arrives won't we," said Dave as he then moved away from the table and Mr Barnes. "I mean it would be quite remiss of us wouldn't you say DC Parsons, to try to begin an interview with out his solicitor being present!"

"Yes, once someone who's in custody requests the presence of a solicitor. No interview may take place until the said solicitor is actually present, sir," said Sam with a half smile.

"Ok officer, you'll have to take him back to the cells until his brief arrives," said Dave as he and Sam left the interview room and headed off along the corridor.

"What were you going to ask him anyway sir?" asked Sam sounding quite curious.

"Ah yes, well to be honest with you, I only had him brought here because he pissed me off back at his company when all he could ask about was the money. I mean, not once did he ask about the health of his staff, not once. So I thought that a little time sitting in a cell on his own might give him an idea what those poor bastards had to go through!" said Dave as they entered their office.

"Sir, there's a note on your desk to get in touch with Stuart green as a matter of urgency," said one of the office staff as Dave entered the room.

"If it was that urgent, then why didn't he call me on my mobile?" said Dave taking out his phone from his pocket. Oh shit, the battery is dead; I must have forgotten to charge it up last night."

Dave, after realising his error, reached for the phone on his desk and dialled the number for Stu.

"Hi Stu, sorry for being unavailable but my phone battery is dead, anyway what's so important?" said Dave.

"Funny you should mention dead batteries," replied Stu with a quip in his voice. "You see when we removed the men's bodies from the van; we discovered their mobile phones under their seats. We were hoping that they had managed to take a picture or something like that prior to them being put inside that metal coffin. Unfortunately, everyone of their phones batteries are dead, so we'll have to wait until we can charge them up enough to see if there is anything useful on them or not!"

"How long will that take?" asked Dave, who was obviously eager to find out what was on them.

"Say about an hour or maybe a little longer to make sure," replied Stu.

"Say Stu, doesn't those vans have onboard security footage built in for just this type of event?" asked Dave.

"Oh yes and that was what I wanted you to come down and see it for yourself," replied Stu. "I think that what little footage there is will give you a useful insight to what occurred on that fateful day."

"Right, we'll be down straight away," said Dave hanging up the phone. "Come on Sam, Stu's got some footage for us to view from the security van and he says that it could be interesting."

Down in the forensic lab, Stu was waiting for them to arrive. He'd already fixed up a screen and projector so that he could run the tape taken from the van's recorder.

"Come on you two, take a pew and see what's on here," said Stu as he switched off the lights and started the player.

The white screen in front of them flickered for a few seconds then they were able to see the view looking through the windscreen from inside the front of the van. On it they could clearly see that in front of the van were the open doors of the huge container.

"What that?" said Sam leaning forward hoping to see the screen better. "It looks like, yes it is. It's a man walking backwards towards the van and it looks as though he's pulling something from within the container. Oh, now he's ducked down and could be attaching whatever it was to the front of the van."

"Is there no sound on the tape at all?" asked Dave feeling very frustrated.

"Unfortunately no," said Stu. " I believe that these are very old tapes and the recording system that's inside the van could even be older than they are."

"Look, there's the side view of one of the men from inside the front of the van," said Dave. "He appears to be looking at someone or something that's to the right of the van. Look, even when the van begins to be winched into the container, he never once takes his eyes of whatever was there. Oh my god, look, this is where they suddenly realise that they're trapped. Jesus Christ, they're trying to open the doors, but as we now know, it was a useless effort on both of their parts. This must be where the doors on the container are being closed; you can just make out the anguish written on the men's faces as they realise that they are about to be locked in with no possible way for them to escape."

"And that's the end of the tape as it must have automatically stopped recording when the light was lost," said Stu as he walked across and switched the lights back on.

"What would have made those men remain inside that van when they knew that they were being dragged inside that container?" said Dave. "If that had been me, I'd have rather taken my chances and tried to leg it from whatever or whoever was out there, I'm afraid even if they had guns, being killed quickly is far more preferable to dying slowly like they all did. God I do hope that there is something on one or more of them mobiles that will help us to catch the bastards that did this to those men."

"And the woman," said Sam.

"Oh bloody hell yes, the woman. Have you been able to find anything more out about her?" said Dave.

"Sorry, all I can tell you is that she was in her early thirties and she'd given birth at least once, but that was a few years ago. There were no signs of injury and I subsequently diagnosed her death was due to suffocation just like the three men," said Stu. "There was no foreign forensic data or fingerprints found anywhere that could indicate who was responsible for this crime. In fact, I'd go as far as to say. If you hadn't discovered the container, then this would have been the perfect crime!"

"If there's one thing I enjoy more than anything," said Dave smiling broadly. "And that is to hunt bastards like these are down and see then put away for a very long time. I sometimes wish that they would put up a fight when we try to arrest them. So that having to restrain them allows me to stretch and twist the long arm of the law more than usual and with a lot more force!"

Stu nodded that he understood what Dave was saying, even if he didn't agree with him some of the times. This time however, was not one of those times.

"Let me know when we can see what's on those phones a.s.a.p." said Dave as he patted Stu on the shoulder as he and Sam left the lab.

———————

14

It was mid afternoon when Mr Barnes solicitor Mr Kieran Blewitt, finally arrived at the Yard. He was immediately allowed time with his client, prior to DCI Geraint being informed that they were ready to comply with his requested interview. On entering the interview room, Dave and Sam were face with both Mr Barnes and his solicitor from across the table.

As Dave made his way across to the table, Sam went and switched on recording equipment. This then emitted a loud bleep, indicating to all, that from now on, whatever was said within the confines of the room would be recorded. As soon as Sam returned to the table, both he and Dave pulled up a chair and sat down.

Dave and Sam both gave their names for the tape, quickly followed by the solicitor and finally by Mr Barnes.

"My client has informed me that you have arrested him on suspicion of hijacking and four counts of murder," said Mr Blewitt. "I wish to say on the record that my client vehemently denies having anything to do with any of the said crimes."

"Noted," replied Dave looking directly at the suspect. "Firstly I would like you to tell me where you were on the day of the hijacking of one of your vehicles?"

"I've already told you that I was at home all day, and no, I don't have anyone who can confirm that!" said Mr Barnes.

"Ok then how come you didn't seem surprised that the crew of the hijacked van were all discovered dead?" asked Sam changing the track of questioning.

"Err, well when they weren't found earlier, it's can happen when something like that goes wrong, doesn't it?" replied Mr Barnes.

"So you are aware that the hijacking went wrong then?" said Dave butting in.

"No, I just meant that it must have, mustn't it for the crew to have all been killed the way they were?" said Mr Barnes, who was by now becoming a little flustered.

"And how were they killed then?" asked Sam.

"Err, I think you're trying to trap my client," butted in Mr Blewitt.

"Ah yes but he's just indicated in front of you that he knew how the men in the vehicle all died. Which is something that we've never told him. So can he inform us how is it that he already knew that?" said Dave, once more looking directly at Mr Barnes trying to keep up the pressure on him.

Dave and Sam watched their suspect physically begin to squirm about in front of them. It was interesting watching him look from Dave to his solicitor and back to Dave. He appeared to be in some sort of a quandary as to what to say next. Then he whispered something in the ear of his solicitor and finally leaned back in his chair and lowered his eyes to look beneath the table.

"My client has asked me to explain where he was for the entire day in question. He has authorised me to explain that he was with someone and is willing to supply you with his contact details," said Kieran Blewitt, as he wrote something down and then passed it across the table towards Dave.

Dave picked up the paper, read what had been written on it then, handed it over to Sam who did the same.

"So are you now telling me that you and this person spent the whole day together?" said Dave.

Mr Barnes with his eyes still averted from the officer's gaze just nodded his head.

"Will you please state your response verbally for the sake of the tape?" asked Dave.

Mr Barnes gave a slight cough to clear his throat and then uttered clearly, "Yes, we were together the entire day."

"Very well," replied Dave. "However, it still doesn't answer how you say you know how the crew were killed. So before we can go any further, I require you to tell me the answer to that one question?"

"Look, when I said that I knew how they had been killed, what I really meant to say was that I assumed that they had either been shot or beaten around the head and it had been those injuries that had eventually resulted in their deaths. So if they didn't die that way, tell me, how did they meet their end?" asked Mr Barnes, but unlike the last time they had spoken, he this time seemed to be genuinely interested in the answer.

Dave took a deep breath and then looked at him and said in a clear and concise tone of voice. "They were somehow forced inside a large sea going metal container while still inside their vehicle and the door to the container were then closed locking them all inside. The container was then placed into a deep hole and the entire thing was covered in soil burying them beneath the ground. As a result, they all slowly suffocated!"

"Oh my God, that's horrendous, who could or would do something like that just to steal the money they were carrying?" said Mr Barnes shaking his head in total disbelief.

"Ah but you haven't heard the strangest part of the nightmare yet," said Dave with a deep sigh.

"What you mean there's more!" said Mr Barnes who was by now leaning forward onto the table obviously eager to learn more.

"Yes," replied Sam taking some of the pressure off Dave. "It's the money, after going through all that and killing all those people. When we opened the van, we discovered that all the money was still in the safe. They never took any of the money, so what was the real reasoning behind all that carnage?"

"Those poor men," said Mr Barnes who was by this time almost disconsolate.

"Ok Mr Blewitt, your client will be released pending on how quick we are able to confirm his whereabouts with the name of the person written on this piece of paper," said Dave as he and am stood up. Then soon after Sam had switched off the recording equipment, they both left the room. As they made their way along the corridor, Dave asked Sam to phone Mr Barnes alibi and if it checks out then to release him.

15

After an hour or so and two mugs of hot coffee later, the phone on Dave's desk suddenly rang out. After answering it, Sam heard Dave say, "Ok Stu we're on our way right now!"

Dave then stood up as he replaced the receiver and told Sam that they were needed downstairs now by Stu in forensics. At the door the lab, Stu met them and appeared to be very excited.

"What you got for me doc?" said Dave as he and Stu came together.

"Well, remember those mobiles that we found inside the van with the flat batteries."

"Yes, you were going to try to charge them up or something like that," replied Dave.

"Well we have and what we found on them is both exciting but very disturbing at the same time," said Stu as he went over to his laptop.

"I've managed to copy all the data from all three phones and have transferred it onto my laptop hoping to make the pictures and sound a little clearer. "Well here goes!"

Stu pressed the play button and the laptop screen lit up. The picture that was on the screen was looking through the van driver's side window. To the side of the roadway they could just make out the figure of a man that had a female on her knees in front of him facing the van.

"What are they saying?" said Dave getting nearer to the screen trying to hear them speak.

"Oh I'm sorry," replied Stu as he leaned across and pressed a few keys bringing the sound up louder. "There, that's as high as it'll go I'm afraid."

"Play that last part again so that this time we can hear what they were saying," said Dave.

Stu tried his best but once again, the sound quality was still too poor for them to hear clearly.

"Is there no way for the techno boys to enhance the sound quality for us," asked Dave hopefully.

"That is after they've had a go at it I'm afraid," replied Stu. "However, what I did do was to ask a friend of mine who teaches deaf people to lip read at one of the colleges in London. If she would agree to translate, what was being said? She willingly agreed and we've had it written down like a script to a play. So, if we watch the picture again, I will then pause, it from time to time and then read out what she has told me they are saying to each other."

Once again, they began to watch the picture. On the small screen it showed that through the driver's side window, the men inside the van could clearly see that there was a man, in his mid thirties dressed in what looked like dark trousers and dark matching shirt standing outside standing behind a female who was at this time kneeling on the floor facing the van. He appeared to be holding the female by her hair with what looked like a handgun pressed against the side of her head.

"Right I'll pause it just there and read what she has put down."

"All of you must stay inside the vehicle or she dies right here in front of you. Sterling, you've already ruined my life after what you did to her, now you're going to have to pay the price. If any of you try to escape then I'll not only kill her but I'll shoot your kid as well!"

"What kid is he talking about and where the hell is it now?" asked Dave.

"Hang on there's some more to come yet," said Stu, as he continued reading."

"In a minute, someone will be hooking up your van to a winch. Then you will be winched inside that container for a short while as a punishment for what you did. If you resist in any way, then her and her kid never see the sunrise tomorrow, do you understand?"

"Right now we will have to watch some more of the pictures so that we can understand what happens next," said Stu.

He pressed play again and everyone's eyes were transfixed to the screen.

This time they watched as the camera on the phone scanned around just in time to see the shape of a man walking backwards out of the container and he looked as though he was pulling something behind him. Then when he was in front of the van, he then crouched down as he turned, preventing anyone from seeing his face and appeared to be connecting something to the front of the van. Then he seemed to disappear from view because the camera suddenly returned to focus on the couple at the side of the road. The man with the gun then said something and gesticulated towards the front of the container. He then produced what looked like a TV remote and aimed it towards the opening. It was just after that, the picture started to jolt about making the picture go a little fuzzy at times. There was a lot of tooing and froing from inside the front of the cab as the van began to enter the opening of the container. Then it looked as though the van itself was being vibrated harshly because the picture began to shake almost uncontrollably, then the picture began to fade due to the lack of light inside the container.

"Let's pause it there and replay it as I once again while I read out her transcript," said Stu.

"You think you could father a daughter with my wife and get away with me not finding out. Well the sluts told me about you fucking her regularly, while I was working all hours God sends, to earn some money for them. Then she told me how she became pregnant and it was your idea to pass the child off as being mine. Well now I know that she's not mine but yours, you'll all have to pay the ultimate price for that deception won't you. It's just a shame that the others have to die as well as you. But I'll leave you to explain that to them."

"Well most of what we've seen on the mobile phones has confirmed what had been recorded on the vans video. But who was the man and the woman in the picture, was he wearing what looks like a uniform? At least we now know that the man all this was being aimed at was Tom Sterling," said Dave. "But why did the other men all have to die, just because of his wife's infidelity."

"Oh hang on there's even more to come and I'm going to save the last piece right until the end," said Stu, with a twinkle in his eye. "That was all we could get from the men's phones at the front of the van. However, this is what was recorded as a follow up on the phone of the man trapped in the rear. From all accounts he was able to take these pictures through the peephole located at the rear of the van for him to identify who was standing outside when collecting or delivering cash."

Once again, the screen lit up but this time it showed the view from the rear of the van looking out through the open doors. It clearly showed the man almost dragging the woman by her arm towards the opening of the container. In his other hand, he still held onto the gun as he violently forced the woman inside. The man then looked as though he took the time to pause for a brief second to gloat at what he'd done. Then he just looked down at the woman, who was by this time lying on the floor just inside the container, looking and pleading with him to let her go Then with an evil grin, he closed both of the doors, sealing all their fates!

"Now this time with the words," said Stu.

"Get inside your fucking coffin you hoar, maybe you can fuck them all before you die."

"Please, please, let her go. Don't put her in here with me to die, it's not her fault. Anyway, I've told several times, she's your child not anyone else's, why won't you believe me?"

It was then that the man closed the door, without saying another word.

"Phew, what a bastard, I mean even if she had been screwing around, to do that to her and those men of which two of them were totally innocent, is just too horrific to think of!" said Sam.

"Ok then Stu, What's this special thing that you've kept till last then?" said Dave wide eyed.

"Well on the last picture of the man when he pushed the woman inside the container, one of the techno boys was able to pick out a couple of things that might help you to identify the killer, well maybe one of them anyway. If you look at these blown up picture's you'll see that on the man's right wrist he is wearing what looks like a silver divers watch and a big one to boot. Above the watch on his forearm, there's a small tattoo of what appears to be a rose. Find those two together and you'll have your man!" said Stu as he handed the pictures over to Dave.

"It's got to be one of those men from the security company, I'm positive of that, Let's get back down there and check all their arms then at least we will be able to either find our murderer, or at least prove that he doesn't work there after all!" said Dave.

16

Pulling up outside the Barnes Security Company, Dave and Sam wasted no time entering the building and headed directly to the office of Robert Barnes the owner. Dave knocked on his door and without waiting, opened the door and walked straight in.

"Oh just barge in why don't you," spouted Mr Barnes, from behind his desk, obviously still upset about his treatment earlier. "What have you come to arrest me again?"

"That depends," replied Dave unemotionally, as he moved closer to him. "I need you to roll up your sleeves so that we can take a look at your arms."

"Why should I?" demanded Mr Barnes folding his arms in a childish protest.

"Look, we don't need you to piss us about; we now know how to identify the person that killed you men. If necessary, we'll force you to show us your arms, but it would be a lot quicker and easier if you did it on your own," said Dave as he began to reach out for his arm.

"Oh, ok then if you think it that important," replied Mr Barnes with a huff in his voice. Then he took of his jacket and rolled up his sleeves to reveal two clear apart from hairy forearms.

"Tell me, do you were a watch?" asked Dave.

"Err, no, I use the one on my mobile why?" replied Mr Barnes, who was by this time quickly becoming curious by these types of questioning.

Dave ignored his question and moved towards the office door saying, "Look, tell me, are Brown and Sterling on duty in the control room today?"

"Yes I believe so," replied Mr Barnes standing up. "But why do you want to know that?"

"There's no time to explain that to you right now," replied Dave opening up the office door and stepping into the corridor. "Will you take us down there and get us inside without giving either of them prior knowledge that were here."

"Yes I can but they will have already seen you arrive on the security camera's that cover the front of the building," said Mr Barnes as he headed the trio as they made their way along the narrow corridor that led eventually to the company's control room.

Outside the door to the control room, Mr Barnes pressed the security buzzer and looked up at the camera for the staff inside to check who was outside prior to the electrically operated door, being released allowing them admittance. On entering the room, Dave immediately noticed that only Simon Hewitt was in there.

"Where's Peter Conway?" asked Dave, "Is he in the loo?"

Simon hesitated and appeared to be reticent in answering Dave's question.

"Look Simon before we go any further, I need you to show me your arms," said Dave as he went across and stood in front of Simon.

Simon, with Dave and Sam now standing in front of him nervously rolled up his shirtsleeves. Then he proceeded to show both sides to them.

"Is that the normal watch you wear?" asked Sam.

"It's the only one I have," replied Simon who was by this time, looking very uncomfortable.

"Ok, you're in the clear, now where's Peter, and don't fuck us about, otherwise you will be going straight from here to Scotland Yard in handcuffs as an accessory to murder!" said Dave as Sam took out his handcuffs from his pocket ready to use them.

"Murder, what murder? I've never even had a parking ticket and you're talking about charging me with murder!" said Simon getting very agitated.

"Look, we've got to know were Peter is and I mean now, otherwise you know what is going to happen to you!" said Dave in his harshest authoritarian tone of voice.

"Ok, he's gone," replied Simon almost hyperventilating. "When we saw you pull up outside the front of the building on the camera's, He suddenly got up and told me that he needed to leave for a few minutes and for me to cover for him. Look, there he is on camera two in the car park getting into his car."

Dave and Sam looked up at the monitor and watched as their main suspect drove off in his car and disappeared from sight.

"Do you have his car registration on record?" said Dave to Simon.

Simon stood up and went across to where the control room logbooks were kept and returned with one of them and handed over to Dave.

"Everything is in alphabetical index," said Simon as he handed the log over to Dave.

Dave then passed it on to Sam and told him to put out an alert for Sterling car. While he was doing that, Dave turned to Simon and asked, "Do you know if Peter has any tattoos on his arms?"

"Yes I think he's got a flower, I think it might even be a rose on one of them," replied Simon who was by this time beginning to calm down.

"Mm, would you know if Peter wear's a wrist watch and if he does, what type of watch it is?" asked Dave.

"He does wear one," replied Simon almost immediately. "What the make is however, I've no idea, all I know is that it's one of those chunky diver's watches or something like that, if that's any help to you,"

"Yes, that's just what we needed to hear," said Dave with a smile, "One last thing; would you have any idea where he might be going to?"

"No not really, I think his wife's left him so he wouldn't be going to stay with her. He did speak about a brother he had one time, but where he lives, I've no idea, sorry!" said Simon. "Err, can I ask, am I still going to be in trouble with you sir?"

Dave glared back at Simon with ice-cold eyes for a few moments, then he relaxed his gaze and replied, "No, but you might be called to give evidence along with your boss at a later stage."

"Phew, I can certainly handle that!" replied Simon as a brief smile crept across his face.

"Right then Mr Barnes, I am going to need you to keep all those log books safe, in case they are called to be used for evidence in a court of law," said Dave. "So you'll need to guard them with your life, so to speak, otherwise you'll have some explaining to do to the judge, won't you?"

Dave and Sam then left the building and returned to their police car. "Right, now we need to try and locate the brother of our suspect, unfortunately for us, we've only got a surname to work with!" said Dave as they climbed inside the car and headed off back to the Yard.

17

The journey back to the Yard was rather quite. Although they now had a solid suspect, he'd beaten them, by making good his escape prior to them arresting him. On the journey, Sam called the office and asked them to enter the name of Conway into the DVLA system and see if their suspect's brother has a driving licence or not.

By the time they reached their office, there was a long printout waiting for them in Dave's in tray! Dave picked it up and he discovered that it was over four A4 pages long.

"Bloody hell I didn't think there would be this many Conway's in the country with driving licences," said Dave shaking his head in dismay.

"Yeh, well all we need to know is do any of them live in or around London," said Dave. "Any further away and we'll have to rely on the local copper's to do the leg work."

After lots of phone calls and a couple of coffee refills, Sam suddenly piped up, "I think this one could be a hot favourite,"

"Why what have you found?" said Dave putting down his mug of coffee.

"Well here's a Sean Conway, he lives in London and according to the DVLA's records, he also has a HGV licence," said Sam.

"We now need to find out where he's working at the present along with his registered home address," said Dave.

"His address is here, along with the licence details," said Sam, "However, I'll make enquiries and discover where he's working at the moment before we get too excited, ok!"

Dave gave him a nod and proceeded to call some of the other names he had on his half of the list of names, while Sam made further enquiries.

"I think this time we've found our man!" said Sam leaning back in his chair. Get this, Sean Conway aged forty-eight and single and works at a mobile crane firm as a driver. The very same firm, is would you believe it, only the same one, that had one of its cranes borrowed and then returned the other day, coincidence of what?"

"Bollocks to coincidences, the odds that this isn't the other man on the film, is going to be hard to defend. Added to that, if he does turn out to be the brother of our suspect, I do believe that we've managed to finally discover both of the men involved in this heinous crime. Let's nip over to the firm and get some conformation that he is Peter's brother before we get any other people involved, shall we," said Dave.

It took them, twenty minutes to reach the crane company where they suspected their suspects, brother worked. From outside the premises parked on the roadway, the two detectives covertly observed the goings on, inside the compound where the cranes were kept.

"Blimey, there's some bloody big blokes in there," said Sam as he watched and counted how many people he could see. "Well I make it nine men I've seen walking about in there, how about you sir?"

"Yeh, about that," replied Dave with his eyes firmly fixed on the yard in question. "But it's not only the size of the men that concerns me, take a look alongside the hut to the right of the crane and tell me what you can see?"

Sam moved forward slowly in the front of the car, so as not to attract any unwanted attention. Then after scanning the yard several times, he suddenly sighed and uttered, "Shit, they've also got dogs in there!"

"Yes and they look like they could be American pit bulls too, and they can be nasty bastards normally, but if they've been trained as guard dogs then they'll be ten times worse," said Dave taking out his mobile. I was going to request that we have a dog section enter the yard with us. However, even our police dogs would stand no chance against bruisers like them. So I'm going to up the ante!"

Thirty minutes later, two vehicles approached Dave's car and pulled up behind. Dave got out and went and had a word with the people inside. Then he returned to his car and said to Sam, "Right let's go and have a word with them shall we?"

"But who are them in those cars?" said Sam looking behind at the two cars.

"Look, don't look behind from here on, the fucking dogs and men that control them are going to be in front of you and you shouldn't be turning you're back on either of those, should you?" said Dave as he placed his hand on Sam's shoulder and urged him forward. "You don't have to worry about your back, I've got yours and mine well covered. But whatever happens inside, I need you to look confident, stand by me and resist the urge to run for cover, understand?"

That last statement from Dave, which was said and intended to instil a feeling of confidence in Sam unfortunately had the opposite effect and he began to wonder what he was now walking into?

As they walked through the open gates into the huge dirt covered yard, they were immediately greeted by the barking and growling from two powerful dogs. That in turn warranted investigation by two men leaving a wooden shed.

"What do you want?" called one of the men dressed in oily jeans and wearing a grimy coloured off white singlet vest.

"I'm DCI Geraint and I'm looking for a Mr Sean Conway that works here?"

"And why would you want to have a talk with him?" replied the man as the other man made his way across to where the two dogs were tied up.

"I'm looking for his brother Peter and I was wondering if he knew where I could find him, that's all!" said Dave who by this time had brought their forward motion to an abrupt stop.

"Look copper, you and your kind, ain't welcome here understand, now fuck off both of you, before we release the dogs and you wouldn't want that now would you?"

"Oh so I take it that they are trained attack dogs then?" said Dave in quick reply.

"Yes and as soon as my mate here unclips their leads then you'll be certain to be on their menu, bon appetite boys," said the man as he gestured to his mate to release the dogs.

"Oh dear, in that case," said Dave as he raised his hand in the air.

Bang, bang!

The sound of two single gunshots rang out from behind the two detectives making Sam jump and shake at the same time. In an instant, Dave and Sam had watched in some trepidation, as the attack dogs, were released by their owners and headed towards them. Then a split second later the two shots rang out and both of the dogs dropped to the ground like stones, after being shot and killed by police marksmen. Before either Dave or Sam could react to the situation, armed police officers fanned around and in front of them.

"Armed police, we have the entire compound surrounded, so do not try to escape. I want you all to put your hands above your heads and move across to that officer over there."

After everyone had been searched and the compound declared safe, Dave went up to the man that had originally confronted them on arrival and asked.

"Right then now perhaps you'll tell me who and where Sean Conway is, otherwise everyone here will be taking a trip down to Scotland Yard and this entire compound will be searched for stolen property or illegal contraband. It's up to you either way will do in my eyes," said Dave shrugging his shoulders.

At first, there was no response from any of the men, then suddenly thick set a man with cropped hair dressed in grubby jeans and t/shirt, stepped forward and said, "I'm Sean Conway, I'm the brother of the guy you're looking for."

"Bloody hell, his arms are bigger than my legs!" whispered Sam.

"Well it's a good job he isn't using them for running then isn't it!" replied Dave, speaking out of the corner of his mouth.

Dave walked to him and asked, "If your, his brother, then you'll know his Christian name and where he works then, won't you?"

"Yeh of course I do, his names Peter and he works for Barnes Securities in the control room."

"Right then Sean, oh is it ok if I call you that," asked Dave. "I'll need you to accompany me to the Yard to answer a few questions, alright?"

"Why can't you ask the questions here?" said Sean defensively.

"Well to be quite honest with you Sean, our presence wasn't really wanted so keeping all your workmates here under armed guard would be a little over the top wouldn't you think," replied Dave calmly.

"Are you putting me under arrest?" asked Sean stepping back from Dave.

"No, why should I, all I need you to do is to come along with us back to the Yard and answer questions about your brother that's all. However, Sean seeing that our arrival here was unwelcome along with the subsequent killing of the two dogs. I feel it could only alienate your colleagues more should we remain here too long. I am however, going to have to place you in cuffs just for the journey you understand, just for the safety my officers. When you get to the Yard, they will be removed allowing you to a little more freedom, ok," said Dave.

So with eyes watching what was happening, Dave asked Sam to apply the cuffs to Sean. Initially, he tried to resist, heightening the tension inside the compound. But when he could see his friends and workmates all looking down the gun barrels of edgy police officers, he decided to comply and allowed Sam to cuff him. Dave and Sam then escorted him out of the compound and placed him in the rear of their car. Sam climbed into the back of the car with him, while Dave waited for the last member of the armed police to vacate the compound. All was a little tense until the huge doors to the compound were slammed shut preventing either the police from re-entering or the men inside mounting any form of counter attack. With the situation now relaxed, Dave thanked the leader of the police team for a job well done and they both drove off in different directions.

———————

18

The journey back to the Yard from the compound was for the most part uneventful, apart from the occasional complaint from Sean, about the handcuffs cutting into his wrists. This though, was quickly allayed by Sam who had been keeping a close eye on his every move since sitting alongside him in the rear of the car. He told him that the journey would end up taking a lot longer if they had to keep stopping for them to adjust the cuffs all the time. To both Dave and Sam's astonishment, Sean appeared to except that as a good enough reason not to stop.

However, once they were back at the Yard, Dave quickly arranged for extra staff to be on hand outside the room, just in case of there was any trouble, when he interviewed Sean.

Once inside the interview room the handcuffs as agreed were removed. Sean was sat looking across a table, facing Dave. Sam then went and switched on the recording device, which emitted a high-pitched bleep when it began recording. Dave and Sam both gave their names for the tape; Sean, was then asked to do the same.

"First of all Sean, I must ask you if you would like to have a solicitor present while these questions are being asked?" said Dave in a matter of fact manner.

"No, why should I, I ain't done nothing wrong!" replied Sean.

"Ok, now that is out of the way, Sean, I need to ask you whether you know, where your brother Peter is?" said Dave. "I'm surprised that he wasn't working at your place with you, you know driving those huge cranes?"

"No, why should I?" replied Sean. "I haven't seen or spoke to him in weeks. As for the other thing, huh, Peter, drive one of those things, don't make me laugh. He wouldn't even be able to start one never mind drive one, he's fucking useless with anything bigger that a van," scoffed Sean at that thought.

"Ah, well that then causes me and in fact you, a bit of a problem," said Dave. "You see, we are currently looking for your brother in connection with being involved with the hijacking of a security vehicle and the subsequent murder of all its crew, four in all!"

"What, Peter being involved with that sort of thing, you must be fucking barmy if you think that," replied Sean then he thought for a second and said with a smile. "Anyway, what are you talking about, there's only three crew members on one of those security vehicles not four, so you've got your numbers wrong there for a start!"

"Mm, yes you're quite right with your figures," said Dave. "However, there were four bodies found inside that container you and your brother buried in the ground the other day killing everyone inside. Yes, there are only three crewmembers on those vehicles. However, we did discover that the dead body a female had also been locked inside that container. That action alone resulted in her slow agonising death along with the deaths of the three men. So come on man, who was she and where is Peter now?"

"Look, I know nothing about any woman found inside that container. What kind of a man do you think I am?" said Sean defiantly.

"Well we know that it was you that hitched the van up to the winch that dragged it inside the container. You have already told us yourself, that Peter was incapable of handling one of your cranes. That must mean that it had been you that lifted the container up and placed it in the ground with everyone still inside. Then either one or both of you then proceeded to bury it. Either way, you are both going to be held responsible for their deaths," said Dave.

"Oh hold on a mo, yes I might have put the container in the hole for my brother, but I had no idea that anyone was still inside!" said Sean emphatically.

"So you admit that it had been you that attached the winch to the front of the van and watched as it was dragged inside the container?" said Dave.

"Yes."

"Then it was shortly after that when Peter put the female inside and closed the doors," said Dave.

"Well yes it was why are you asking me all this again?" asked Sean.

"Oh I just needed to make sure that I'd got all the facts of the case right inside my head before I went any further. Well with all the evidence that we have and the fact that we've now been able to download all the pictures and video's from all three of the mobile phones, from within the van itself. I'd say that you're well and truly in the shit and your brother has left you to carry the murder rap in place of him," said Dave as he suddenly stood up and faced Sean across the table.

"Sean Conway, I'm now arresting you on suspicion of hijacking and four counts of wilful murder.

"You do not have to say anything. But it may harm your defence if you do not mention when questioned something which you later rely on in court. Anything you do say may be given in evidence. Do you understand?"

"You fucking bastards, you lied to me just to get me here!" shouted Sean as he made a lunge towards Dave and Sam.

Both of the detectives however side stepped his advance and the prisoner fell chest downwards on top of the fixed metal table. So while Dave leaped on top of him pinning him down, Sam ran and pressed the alarm strip that stretches around the entire interview room for such an emergency. As the internal alarm rang out officers that had been previously positioned outside the room, burst in and quickly managed to overpower and subdue the prisoner. He was then handcuffs and re-seated in his chair. This time though with the added precaution of both his arms now firmly attached to the chair, which in turn, was anchored to the floor.

Now with the prisoner firmly secured in his seat and with extra officers on hand to intervene should he become violent, Dave once again resumed his line of questioning.

"Right then Mr Conway, I'll get straight to it," said Dave. "Tell me the truth; was the female that we discovered inside the container, Peter's wife Sonya, yes or no? We know that you must have known that those men were unable to escape from that vehicle as soon as they'd been dragged inside the container. It was obvious because the side of the van was pressing against the sides of the container preventing any such action on their part. So when you put them in that hole, you knew their fates were well and truly sealed!"

Sean didn't reply to Dave's question, he just sat there with his head hung low, totally devoid of any emotion.

"Tell me where Peter is now then, surely that is going to be an easier question to answer than the last one," said Dave.

Once again, Sean refused to answer.

"Ok, then if you're not going to answer any of my questions then I have not option other than to change the original charge of suspicion of being involved with the hijacking and murders of the four people inside the container. To one of hijacking and the wilfully orchestrating and committing the heinous crime of premeditative murder on four counts!" said Dave. "Ok officers, you can take him back to his cell, where he should prepare to make himself comfortable, say for the rest of his life."

With that, half a dozen officers surrounded the prisoner and restrained him while they released his wrists from the chairs anchor points. Dave along with Sam in the meantime made their way out of the interview room and back to their office.

"Have the DVLA make a check to see what type of vehicle Sean has registered to him and put an alert out for it. You never know, it might just give us a lead to where Peter is hiding out!" said Dave.

19

Within an hour of the request being made, details of a 1989 ford transit campervan along with the vehicles registration number, was being placed on to Dave's desk.

"Get this out over the radio, will you Sam. Maybe someone will be lucky enough to spot it parked up somewhere," said Dave as he handed the memo across to Sam.

For a couple of hours there was no word about the missing campervan. Then just like buses, three calls arrived within five minutes. The police control room, first had a nearby police patrol check out each of the sightings to establish conformation before notifying Dave.

Finally, Dave received the conformation he'd been waiting for, about the campervans position.

Which was at the far end of a little used industrial estate, parked up behind some shrubbery. Now that he had that, Dave wasted no time in arranging for a dog patrol and an armed response team to accompany him and Sam to go and facilitate Peter Conway's arrest. Close to where the van was parked up, final arrangement were made prior to the arrest taking place. Dave and Sam were to approach the campervan, after police cars had blocked the front and rear of the van preventing any chance of escape. The dog patrol was to wait to the rear in case the suspect tried to make a break for it. The armed response team were only there in case the suspect decided to use a weapon. Then it would be down to the leader of the team to take control of disarming him. But if the suspect is not armed but still tries to escape, that's when the dog and handler will affect the arrest for him.

As the witching hour arrived, two police cars roared into view then, they screeched to a stop expertly positioning their vehicles at either end of the campervan. The officers then withdrew to a safe distance, bearing in mind the fact that a handgun had been seen to be used on the videos. Now it was Dave's turn to approach the van's side door.

"Peter Conway, this is DCI Geraint from Scotland Yard. The campervan is completely surrounded, so I want you to come out with your hands above your head," said Dave in a loud but concise tone of voice.

At first, there was no response from Conway or any sign of movement coming from inside the van. Then someone shouted out from inside the van.

"I've got a gun in here, so if anyone comes through that door, I'll blow their fucking head off, d'you hear me copper?"

"Yes I hear you Peter," replied Dave calmly. "However, I should point out to you that any use of a firearm would result in members of the armed response team undertaking the arrest!"

An eerie silence then fell across the area, then in an instant, the door to the campervan flew open. The suspect emerged in the doorway holding a handgun and waving it wildly above his head.

"Come near me coppers and you'll all die," shouted Conway as he began to run towards Dave and Sam.

Bang!

A single shot rang out hitting the suspect in his right gun arm making him drop the weapon on the ground. Then a police dog ran in and hit him hard from the left side, grabbing hold of his left arm and knocking him down onto the floor. As Conway struggled to try to free himself from with the powerful dog's jaw. The only audible sound that could be heard over his screams, was the sound of the police dog growling and biting down hard onto the suspect's remaining good arm. Dave gave a wry smile as he watched the suspect struggle to escape the dogs ever tightening grip and he thought briefly, about how those poor people must have struggled in vain to escape from the metal coffin, this excuse for a human being had put them in. Seconds later, the dog handler moved in to remove his dog and place the man in handcuffs.

Dave then moved closer to the now prisoner and looked him straight in the face and said,

"Peter Conway, I'm arresting you for hijacking a security vehicle and for the wilful murder.

"You do not have to say anything. But it may harm your defence if you do not mention when questioned something which you later rely on in court. Anything you do say may be given in evidence."

Do you understand the charge?"

"You've got nothing on me, so I'm saying nothing to you ok!" replied Conway, staring straight back at Dave in defiance.

"Ok, lads, take him back to the Yard and arrange for this campervan to be towed to the police compound," said Dave.

Back at Scotland Yard, Dave and Sam prepared themselves for the interview with Conway. Dave already knew that he would not make their task of proving his guilt easy, so he readied himself for the long haul.

Conway was already waiting in the interview room when Dave and Sam finally arrived. The flesh wound on his arm from the gun shot and the dog bite on his other arm had both been treated by a paramedic and neither deemed not to be life threatening.

On entry to the room, they were greeted by Conway who was by this time dressed in an all in one white outfit that looks just like a giant baby grow. He was not in there alone but was accompanied by two police officers, who's only input in these proceedings would take place if the prisoner should decide to turn violent.

As before, Dave made his way towards the table where Conway was sitting, while Sam went and switched on the recording machine. As soon as the high-pitched bleep sounded, they knew that everything in that interview room, was now being recorded.

Dave and Sam then said their names for the tape and asked Peter to do the same. Unfortunately, he refused to speak and just shook his head in defiance. Dave then spoke the prisoners name for the tape, and asked him if he would like to have a solicitor present during the interview. Once again, he refused to answer Dave's question and shook his head.

"Ok then Peter, I've asked you if you wanted a solicitor present and in front of these witnesses, you responded by a shake of your head. So I'm taking that as a no so allowing the interview to proceed. First things first just so that we're clear on something. Why did you force your wife inside that container with the security van and leave her to die like that," asked Dave calmly.

Once again, Peter refused to answer but just sat there smiling.

Ok then let's try to look at this from a different perspective. Why is it that you can't you father children of your own and your wife has to go look elsewhere for a real man to satisfy her needs?" said Dave, this line of questioning brought wide eyes from Sam and the two officers standing guard. "I mean, how old are your wife's kids no? Oh they must be around eight and five, I'd imagine, so you've been paying for them to go on holidays and school trips, I mean the clothes bill alone must be quite large. How did you feel when you were told that they weren't yours but one of your close friend and workmates. I bet you began to think about all the snide remarks that the men in the company were making about how good your wife was to one of them. Or were there more I wonder?" said Dave ,as he watched Conway's face begin to get redder and redder, as the fury deep inside of him began to boil over to the surface.

Then finally, Conway snapped and tried to lunge forward towards Dave but his arm restraints that firmly anchored him to his chair prevented that from happening.

"You bastard, talking to me like that," shouted Conway as he seethed aggression through his teeth. "If I didn't have these things on then things would be different and those fucking excuses for coppers wouldn't be able to stop me either."

"Ah but you see, you're only good when you are in charge of the situation. Like when you held the gun to your wife's head to ensure that the men inside the vehicle didn't get out and kick your arse. They only remained in that van in the hope that your wife wouldn't be harmed. But when you knew that they were trapped, you forced inside the container with them anyway. I mean, a woman is going to be no match for a big macho man like you is she," said Dave straight-faced and virtually unblinking.

Conway stared for a while at Dave and then smiled and said, "You're bluffing, you have no proof that I was involved with any crime, have you copper?"

"Well you see that's where you're wrong, I'm afraid," replied Dave. "You see, we have the onboard camera that recorded what happened to the men in the security van. The most damning video however came from the men's own camera phones. You see, even as they were being forced inside that container, they continued recording what was going on outside. They have your brother Sean hooking them up to the winch and you threatening your wife with a handgun. The clincher however, was the clear picture of the man's arm that forced the woman into the container prior to him closing the doors.

You see, on that final few frames, it clearly showed the man's diver's watch and the tattoo of a rose on his forearm!"

That last statement had a profound effect on Conway, as he looked down and instinctively reached across and slid up his sleeve, to reveal the tattoo of a rose on his arm. "A watch and a fucking tattoo, that's all you've got?"

"Yes, oh and don't forget the body of your wife that was discovered inside the container," said Dave smugly. "Oh at least you can tell me now where the two children are?"

"Why should I care where they are, they're not mine, she told me that, so if there not mine then there not my responsibility are they? If you want to know where they are, then you go and look for them," replied Conway with a wide grin on his face.

"So am I to understand that you staged this charade of murder under the guise of a hijacking, when in reality it was a domestic problem that got way, out of hand. Tell me, did you bury the container hoping that it would never be found?" said Dave trying to find out how this man's mind was working.

"If the van disappeared and was never found, it would have eventually been forgotten. If a wife decides to sod off from her husband and disappear, then eventually even she would have been forgotten too. So I thought why not kill two birds with one stone, get rid of an unfaithful wife and the bastard that was screwing her at the same time, simple!" said Conway, almost sounding relieved that it was finally over.

"Ok, I'm going to stop this interview now, while we go and try to find those missing children before it's too late," said Dave standing up. "Officers, you can take Mr Conway back to his cell now."

Sam switched off the recording machine and followed Dave out of the room. "Christ, you're like Jekyll and Hyde in there sir. I thought that the onetime his chair was coming off the floor, when he tried to lunge at you."

"Yes me too, but that's what those two coppers were therefore," replied Dave smugly.

20

"Well, what did you think about that then?" said Dave. "Is he a cold fish or what?"

"He's not cold he must be made of ice. I can, in a way understand someone killing that way when there are strangers involved. But how does someone do that to members of his own family?" said Sam.

"Mm, what concerns me, now is where the hell are those two children now?" said Dave as he reached across and picked up his phone.

"Coffee," said Sam standing up.

"Oh yes please," replied Dave as he briefly interrupted what he was saying.

On Sam's return, armed with two hot mugs of coffee, Dave told him that he'd put in a request to the control room and the social services that he is informed, if any children are discovered abandoned, anywhere in the London area.

"Will you be accused of bullyboy tactics when Conway's brief hear what was said in the interview?" asked Sam.

"Might do, but then he was offered the services of a solicitor but he declined. Anyway, what did I say that was incorrect, I mean to say, all I was asking is how he feels knowing that his friend and workmate had screwed his wife. Now even he's verified that actually happened so me saying something that he was already aware of cannot in my mind, be construed as using bullyboy tactics," replied Dave confident in his actions. "Oh we must remember to get the names of those officers that were present in the interview room when he refused the option of a solicitor."

"Already done sir," said Sam with a smile.

Just then, the phone rang and Dave reached across and answered it. "DCI Geraint, Mm, oh that's very interesting, right we'll be straight over, thank you."

Dave replaced the receiver and sat back in his chair and said, "That was a Miss Pearson from social services. She tells me that a couple of nights ago a little girl was discovered on a country lane. From all accounts, the driver of a car almost hit her as she stumbled out of the bushes and into the path of his car. She wanted to know if we would like to come and see if she is the missing girl or not. Oh we'd better be sure of both the kid's names before we meet up with her."

"Peter and Mary," said Sam after scanning through his notes. "Peter is eight and his sister is only five."

"Right let's drink up and get over there shall we," said Dave as he downed the last few dregs of coffee.

At the children's home where social services had placed her for her own safety, the two detectives were met at the door by a smart but dowdily dressed female.

"Hello, are you Miss Pearson from social services," said Dave as he offered her his hand.

"Yes, but please call me Fiona."

"Ok Fiona, I'm DCI Geraint and this is DC Parsons, you told me about a little girl found wandering late at night."

"Yes, but please come into this office and I'll tell all that I know about her," said Fiona as she showed them into the hallway and then to an empty office. "She was almost knocked down by a couple who were driving home in the early hours of the morning. She was icy cold and they wrapped her up, took her to their home and called the emergency services. All she was wearing when they found her was a lightweight summer dress. There were no socks or shoes on her feet, her legs however, were found to be covered in dried blood, from various cuts that covered most of her little legs. Her feet were covered in dirt and also had cuts on them obviously from walking a distance through the woods."

"Do you know her name yet and can we get to see her?" asked Dave.

"To answer your first question, no, we have no idea what her name is. We've tried to get her to tell us but she hasn't spoken since she's arrived here. As for meeting her, yes but I must warn you that she is quite withdrawn and might not respond to you," said Fiona as she gestured the two detectives to follow her.

Don the short corridor, Dave and Sam were then shown into a room that was filled with toys. Over in the corner, sitting on the floor, they saw the shape of a little girl, who was holding onto a doll and rocking back and forth.

"Is that her?" asked Sam who was obviously distressed seeing her acting like that.

"Yes, that's her," replied Fiona. "That's all she's done each day she's been with us here. We've tried to get her to play with some of the other children but she just shuts down when they come near her."

Dave held his hand up to both Fiona and Sam indicating that he wanted them to stay where they were. Then he quietly edged a bit closer to her and when he was about six feet away, he sat down on the floor, picked up a toy train and began to play with it.

"Choo, Choo," went Dave as he pushed the train along the wooden floor. "Uh Oh, it's crashed," said Dave quietly. "Oh well I'll just have to make it better then."

"What's wrong with it?" said a quiet voice.

"I was playing with this train and i pushed it too hard and it fell over," replied Dave keeping his voice as soft and quiet as he could.

Fiona, when she heard the little girl speak for the first time to Dave, gripped Sam's arm and gave it a tight squeeze. "She's actually talking to him, it's amazing!"

Sam tapped her hand to reassure her and gave her a little smile. "He seems to know what he's doing."

"My names Dave, what's your name?"

At first, the little girl didn't respond, so Dave said nothing and just carried on playing with the toy train. "Oh dear, it's fell over again. I'm hopeless at this game; I suppose I'll have to look for something else to play with instead." Dave put the toy train down and sat there silent with his arms folded.

"What are you doing now?" said the little girl again but his time she turned her head slightly to look at Dave.

"Well I keep making the train fall over, so I need to find something else to play with but all the toys are by you," said Dave.

The little girl looked from Dave to the toys and then back to Dave again, who was sitting there with a sad face looking at all the other toys.

"You can come and have some of these if you want to," said the little girl shyly.

"Are you sure that you don't mind?" asked Dave softly.

"No, come on," called the little girl a bit louder to him.

Dave slowly stood up and as the other two watched in silence, he edged closer to where the girl was sitting. "Can I sit here next to you?"

The little girl looked up at Dave and replied with a sigh, "If you want to."

Dave then sat on the floor and began to play with some of the toys. A little while later after they had been playing close to each other, Dave asked without looking at her, "You know my name, why won't you tell me your's?"

The little girl picket up the doll again and squeezed it tight. "I'll go back over there if you don't want to talk to me," said Dave as he began to stand up and move away.

"No, you can stay, my names Mary, why are you here?"

"Oh I have come to help one of the other children that got lost to find their way back home," said Dave, as he picked up a tatty old brown teddy bear and held it tight. "Why are you here?"

Mary turned and looked at Dave to see if he was watching her. But when she saw that he was playing with the teddy bear instead, she seemed to relax and said, "My daddy locked me and my brother Peter inside a shed in the woods then he went away and left us there all alone. Peter broke a window with something he found on the floor. Then he tried to help me climb out of the window but I slipped and cut my legs on some glass. He took off my shoes and socks and wiped some of the blood away, then lifted me up and pushed me through the window and I fell down on some dirty grass. I waited for him to come after me but he called and told me to go and find some help. It was very cold and dark and I was scared of being eaten by animals that live in the trees. The next thing I remember is waking up here. I want to find Peter but I don't know where I left him?"

"Would you like me to look for Peter for you?" said Dave in a soft voice.

"Would you?" asked Mary as she put her doll down for the first time and turned and faced Dave.

"If you like, I could go and have a look for him right now," said Dave, giving Mary a little smile.

"What about helping the other child though?" asked Mary?

"Well my friend Sam over there can stay and do that while I go and try to find your brother, would you like that?" asked Dave.

Mary nodded her head and gave Dave a very strained smile and said," Yes please."

With that, Dave handed the teddy bear to Mary, stood up slowly and walked quietly out of the room closely followed by Sam and Fiona.

"That was marvellous," said Fiona who was obviously ecstatic at the progress that Dave in such a short period of time, had made, where they had failed. "Tell me, is she the missing girl that you've been looking for?"

"Yes and the fact that she has a brother by the name of Peter reaffirm's that fact," said Dave. "Now we must try to locate wherever he might be right now."

"Is there anything that you want me to do for you," asked Fiona, who after what she'd just witnessed, wanted more than ever to help if she possibly could.

"Yes, I need you to make sure that whoever is looking after Mary, takes things nice and slow. She's been through a lot more than a child of her age should and I don't want a spotty face geek to try to rush things and throw her even deeper inside herself."

"You can leave that to me," replied Fiona.

"Now all we have to do is to locate her missing brother, if he's still alive that is!" said Dave shaking his head.

———

21

After leaving the children's home and while Dave gathered his thoughts. Sam got onto the police control room and got them to search through their records for the report of where the abandoned girl, had originally been discovered.

"Right, got it," said Sam. "According to their records, a Mr and Mrs Parker found Mary as they drove home from a party early in the morning. This is their address sir," as he handed the slip of paper across to Dave.

"You drive Sam; I've got to get my head back together after talking to young Mary, what a kid. After all she's been through she still was concerned that she might jump the queue for help ahead of some other child!"

The journey out to where the Parkers live took about twenty minutes. In that time however, Dave managed to close his eyes for most of the trip, not sleeping but trying to slow his brain down to a better working speed.

Outside the Parkers, Dave and Sam stood by the car and took a few seconds to take in the beauty of the idyllic surroundings. Apart from the single-track country lane, the only sounds that were audible were coming from the birds and animals of the wood.

"Wow what a place to live," said Sam. "Fancy being surrounded by tall trees and the myriad of different animals and birds, that call this place home."

"Mm, you what I'm thin king about right now?" said Dave as he looked all around.

"No, what?" replied Sam eager to find out.

"I was just thinking what this place must have looked like to a little girl of five, who was on her own in pitch blackness after being locked in a shed by her own father. She must have been petrified, the poor little cow."

Just then, the front door opened and a smartly dressed female was standing there. "Can I help you," she asked.

"I wonder are you Mrs Parker?" asked Dave politely.

"Yes, why, what do you want?" she asked sounding a little concerned at their presence.

"I am DCI Geraint and this here is DC Parsons. We're here to speak to you about the little girl that you discovered close to here the other night."

Dave and Sam then took out their warrant cards and showed them to the woman. "Oh please, won't you come inside."

As they entered the lounge, Dave shook his head in disbelief at the high standard of furniture that they had in there. It was if everything, had been specially made to fit inside the old style cottage.

"Mrs Parker, all we're interested in knowing is where exactly, did you and your husband find the little girl. I need you to think very carefully because we've reason to believe that her older brother may still be out there," said Dave.

"Erm, I think I know the place but my husband is much better than me at remembering things, I'm afraid," she replied.

"And where is your husband?" asked Sam.

"Oh he's at work in London, he'll be back in about three hours or so though, if you really need to speak to him."

"In those three hours Mrs Parker, that missing child might die. So I really need you to stop and think hard for me. Then I want you to take us to the exact spot where you found her, do I make myself clear!" said Dave who was by now beginning to sound exasperated by her complete lack of response to the whole situation.

Those few strong words from Dave seemed to hit a spot with her and she began to concentrate back to that night. "Ok, I do believe I can remember where it was," she suddenly said to everyone's great relief.

Then they all left the cottage and Dave and Sam followed Mrs Parker back down the winding lane until she suddenly came to a stop. They watched as she got out of her car and had a good look around. "Yes, this is it," she shouted to the two detectives. "I remember, this is exactly where the little girl walked out in front of our car."

"Good for you," replied Dave. "Now this is very important. From which direction was she coming from?"

Mrs Parker then went and sat against the boot of her car and thought hard. "From the left, yes I'm positive that she stumbled in from the left, because we were driving the other way and she almost hit the passenger side of the car. Was that helpful for you?"

"Very helpful Mrs Parker, thank you for working with us like you did," said Dave all the time encouraging her. Now you can leave us here and return to your home. We'll arrange for a search party to sweep this entire area."

So as she turned her car around and disappeared back along the lane, Dave made arrangements for a search team to attend the site ready for the commencement of a search. A little over an hour passed by before vehicles began arriving. Some of them had members of the search team, while others carried vital equipment such as torches and radios the final piece of the jigsaw was the arrival of two dog handlers. Their dogs were special, as they had been trained to search out bodies be they alive or dead.

Dave then briefed the team about what they were going to be looking for.

"Ladies and gentlemen, we are looking for an eight year old boy. We have reliable information that he was last seen locked inside an old shed possibly in this area of woodland. However, whether he's still there or not is another thing. What I do know is that he will by now, be very cold and weak, so time is not going to be on our side with this search. However, that doesn't mean that corners are to be cut just to try and save time," said Dave as he handed the search over to the professionals.

"What do you think the odds of finding him still alive are?" asked Sam.

"It's going to be getting dark soon, so probably slim, but even slim odds are better than none, in my book. I like to think in these situations, imagining a missing person as still being alive, puts more impetus into the search," replied Dave as the search team split up into small groups and headed off into the trees.

———————

22

10pm, the search team had managed to cover almost a quarter of the wooded area. However, none of the team had reported any sign of the missing lad. Then came a call over the radio to say that a girl's pink cardigan had been found hooked up on a thorny bush. Dave asked for the grid location and after finding it on a map, he and Sam made their way there.

The trek through the woods was not easy especially in the dark with only the narrow beam of light to go by. Many times both men had a smack in the head from a rogue tree branch that seemed to reach out in the darkness and hit them as they walked by. Twenty long minutes later, they reached the grid reference and met up with members of the search team.

One of the men handed the small cardigan over to Dave and showed him where he had found it.

It looks as though it must have become snagged on the bush, as she made her way through the trees," said Dave as he looked around for something, anything to indicate which direction she'd come from. Nevertheless, in the darkness only a guess as to which direction to look in would be his best option.

"Do any of you, know of an old shed or woodman's hut anywhere near to here," asked Dave in desperation.

"There used to be one about five hundred yards in that direction," said one of the older members of the search team. "But to be honest with you, the last time I saw it, it was virtually falling down and that must have been at least ten years ago. I might even have already fallen down by now," he added.

"And you are?" said Dave to the man.

"Oh everyone just calls me old Harry because of my grey hair and wiry beard, I suppose."

"Ok Harry, how about you showing Sam and me this old shack, while the rest of the team carry on with their search, just in case it is a waste of time," said Dave.

"That's ok with me," replied Harry. "I hope I can find it again in the dark after all this time."

"Of that, I've no doubt," said Dave with a smile and nod of his head.

As they headed off and quickly disappeared into the darkness the rest of the team continued with their search pattern. The trek to the old shack though, took a fair time due to the dense undergrowth and Harry constantly having to reassess his directional approach. Finally though, the shape of the ram shackled wooden structure appeared in the lights of their torches. The men made their way around to the door and discovered that there was a relatively new padlock anchoring the door shut.

"Why on earth, would anyone in their right mind put a padlock on something so rundown?" said Harry as he tried shaking the door.

"Obviously to keep people out or on the other hand, it could be to keep someone inside?" said Dave as he made his way around to the far side of the hut. There in the light of his torch he found what looked like an old window. The glass however looked as though it had been broken from the inside, because the slivers and shards of glass were on the outside of the hut.

"Around here!" called Dave. as he moved closer to the window. He then waited for Sam to arrive and they both shone their torches through the window at the same time. This allowed them to see the inside of the hut more clearly. At first, all they could see were years of dirt an cobwebs that were mixed up with old bits of broken wood and an a couple of smashed chairs piled up in the corner. It wasn't until their torch lights were being brought back towards the window did they find the body of a young lad.

"Oh God, he's in here," said Dave as he shook his head.

"Is he alive?" asked Harry.

"No," replied Sam as he followed Dave towards the door. "Will you make the call to the team leader Harry and tell him it looks like we've found the missing boy and give him our position."

While Harry got on his radio, Dave gave the door a kick. The door flew open under the kick and the two Detectives carefully entered the hut. Now for the first time, they could see that the missing boy had somehow fallen through the rotten floor.

"It looks as though he had been helping his younger sister to climb out of the window, when the floor beneath him gave way. It then looked as though the splintered wood had pierced the main artery in the inner thigh of his leg, meaning that he bled to death in this God forsaken place," said Dave as he bent down for a closer look at the boy's injury.

"So this is why he never followed his sister out of the window," said Sam. "The poor little sod, I can imagine him calling out to her to go on without him, knowing that he couldn't get out of the hole by himself. I wonder if even at his young age, he knew that he was going to die. How can someone so young comprehend the fact that your own father had put you and your sister this hellhole to die. I mean, how could anyone put children through this type of hell knowing they were going to die all alone!"

"Let's get Stu and his team out here a.s.a.p. so we can get this poor sod out of this place," replied Dave as he had to turn away from such a heart wrenching scene.

As soon as Stuart and his team arrived, Dave had a quick word with him and then he and Sam left them to it.

23

The following morning, Dave arrived at the office early after getting next to no sleep. He found that every time he closed his eyes to sleep, the sight of young Peter trapped in the rotten floor, flashed to the forefront of his thoughts. Not long after he'd got there, Sam appeared all bleary eyed obviously not having had much sleep either.

"Morning Sam," said Dave half-heartedly. "You look like shit!"

"Mm, yes and I feel that way too," replied Sam with a shrug of his shoulders. "Well to be honest with you sir, you don't look much better!"

Dave gave a half smile and said, "Coffee."

"Coffee," replied Sam as he draped his coat across the back of his chair.

Over the next hour, they chatted about the previous day and how things had developed. This had two avenues of thought; one was to help them to put things that had happened in some sort of context. Second, them being able to talk about what they'd seen in private, helped them to come to terms with some of the horrors of their job.

Suddenly Stuart Green appeared in the office doorway. "Morning you two," he said sounding much the worse for the lack of sleep.

"Morning Stu," replied Dave. "Coffee!"

"Oh yes please, good and strong if only to keep my eyes open for a little longer," replied Stu as he pulled up another chair and sat down.

When Sam returned with the liquid tonic, he then began to give them both the gist of his findings concerning the boy that they had found.

"I completed my autopsy and the findings are sad to say the least. The boy did die after piercing a main artery as he fell through the floor. It was from that injury alone that he died, if the wood had punctured his leg an inch either way then, he wouldn't have died that way," said Stu as he gulped down some welcome coffee.

"Is this the lad that was locked in the shed by his father?"

"Yes, along with his younger sister too," replied Dave. "I believe that he fell through the floor helping her to get out through the window!"

"Now that was a brave little soldier, making sure that his sister had a better chance of surviving than he had," said Stu as he put his mug of coffee down and stood up. "I'll let you have my report a.s.a.p."

"Go home and get some sleep Stu. Tomorrow will do just fine as far as I'm concerned," said Dave as he gestured to Stu to leave.

"Oh I nearly forgot to give you this," said Stu as he handed Dave a slip of paper.

Dave looked at it and gave a wry smile, "Are you sure of this?"

"One hundred percent positive!" replied Stu as he made his way out of the office waving his hand in the air.

"What was that sir?" asked Sam curiously.

Dave then flicked the paper across to him and sat back in his chair.

Sam then looked at what was written and he too leant back and shook his head.

"Right, I know it's early but fuck it, let's go and have a chat with Peter Conway in his cell shall we?" said Dave as he wearily stood up and stretched. "Let's make his day start with a bang, aye!"

They both then made their way down to the cells and got the duty sergeant to unlock Peter

Conway's cell for them. As the door opened, they saw that Conway was still fast asleep.

"Wait here Sergeant," said Dave in a loud voice. "This won't take long. Come on Peter, wake up, we've got some important news for you!"

Peter stirred from his deep sleep, swung his legs off the bed and sat up facing Dave. "What the fuck do you want at this time in the morning?"

"Oh we thought that you'd want to know this snippet of information as soon as possible," said Dave as he handed Conway the piece of paper that Stu had given him.

"What the fuck's this then?" demanded Peter as he struggled to read what was written on it.

"That, is the findings of DNA taken from you, you're wife and the two children," said Dave. "It proves that you were their father after all. She never cheated on you and that means that all those people died for nothing more than your own insecurity. Oh and we're adding the charge of Filicide to your charges. If you don't know what that is, then I'll tell you. It's the cold blooded murder of you son Peter. We found where you left those children; your son had though already died after bleeding to death while attempting and successfully saving his sister. Your daughter is safe and now living in a children home.

As Dave watched the door to the cell close, the reality of the situation finally hit home to Conway and he screamed out uncontrollably.

"That felt good," said Dave as he and Sam walked away from the cell with Conway's screams echoing along the whole cellblock.

"Yes, you know funnily enough, I really enjoyed giving him that news," replied Sam. "Now what's on the cards for the rest of the day?"

Two hours later, Dave was back at the children's home, sitting on the floor of the toy room alongside Mary. He knew that somehow it was going to be down to him to try to explain to her that he'd kept his promise to her and had managed to find her brother. Unfortunately, he'd become very poorly before he was found and was now in heaven with their mother. They were both looking down and watching over her a she grows up!

The End

Made in the USA
Charleston, SC
01 August 2011